THE UNFORTUNATE EVENT

&

Other Stories

By

Dido G. Kotile

Also, By

Dido G. Kotile

A Novel

The Lonely Path

ACKNOWLEDGEMENTS

To my family for their support and patience.

To my beta reader: Guyo Kotile, Illustrator, Wasima Farah and editor, Prianka Sachi (Fivver). The Unfortunate Event and Other Stories is better because of your feedback.

Contents

THE IVORY TRACKERS

James Kaya, the chief game warden, sat at his desk flipping through the pages of a report; he paused at the word "Gotu," circled in red.

"The people you mentioned in the report, do you have any evidence?" questioned James, tapping his cigarette lightly over his ashtray.

Golo sat on the other side of the desk; and though his boss' eyes remained on the report, he replied. "Not yet, but I'm working on it."

James frowned, as he removed the report from the pile and stashed it into his briefcase. "There's nothing else that we can do, without evidence. I'm sure you know with whom you're dealing."

Golo knew this, but he hadn't lost hope.

"Still, you did an excellent job."

Golo knew that this was his cue to leave; he got up and walked towards the door, all the while, wondering if his boss was happy or sad about the report.

"They have deserted Gotu area, so I suggest you check the area beyond Shaba," added James, as Golo opened the door, "We need to have everything under control before the tourist season begins."

"Yes, sir."

"Wait," said James; Golo turned back, but moments later, James waved him away and opened the newspaper on his desk, "Never mind, you may go now. I'll talk to you later."

And without waiting for a response, James began reading.

Talk to me later? wondered Golo, as he walked back to the waiting Land Rover.

"Are you ready?" he asked, as he strapped himself in, at the end of the front seat.

Juma winked.

"And you?"

Musa, the driver, nodded but kept his eyes on the office.

"Look who is visiting the station," pointed out Juma, as he motioned his head.

Aziz came out of a car and entered the office.

"He got the contract to build the extensions of the offices," added Musa, eager to appear knowledgeable.

"Okay. Now hit the road."

Musa knew the rugged road well; a trail of dusty wind followed them as they bounced along the well-worn path. Golo remained quiet throughout most of the journey, listening while Musa and Juma talked.

"Eh?" interrupted Golo; he craned his head towards Musa and asked Juma. "What did Musa say?"

"Oh!" replied a startled Juma, "He was saying that the boss intends to transfer one of us to another station."

"A transfer," gasped Golo, surprised, "Who?"

Juma just shrugged.

"One of us."

Half an hour later, Golo instructed the driver to turn towards Gotu area. "From here, we shall go on foot and come back at around three o'clock."

Juma shook his head at Golo's words and opened his mouth, but the driver had already obliged.

And so, their trek on land began. They walked in silence for most of the time, only speaking when they found something important. "Look," said Golo, as he stopped and waved over Juma; footprints crossed their path.

The patchy soil markings were clear; the prints curved and distorted chunks of clods that were indented underneath, short, twisted, flattened, and barely visible grass that formed a part of indelible features.

Golo and Juma followed this path.

Fresh twigs laid scattered on the crippled trail, it's leaves bent from being trampled on. Golo bent lower and studied the scorched and faded vegetation; it was spotted with blood.

"Did you see this?"

Juma looked down at him, nodding.

"Yes," he replied, "There were three."

"Bastards," cursed Golo, looking up at the sky in frustration. The naked afternoon's sun shot it's rays down, filtering through the drooping leaf canopies.

Golo unbuttoned the front part of his green khaki uniform coat, exposing his white vest, which was now bathed in sweat. And now, like a soldier in combat, ready to shoot; he took careful yet defiant strides, prepared for an ugly encounter even though the atmosphere around him remained peaceful.

"Juma," he called out.

Juma looked up, hesitantly.

"Yes."

Golo paused and propped the butt of his rifle on the ground with one hand, while, holding a canister of water with the other. Flipping the lid, he sipped the water before splashing some on his face. Juma reached for the water and emptied it in one turn.

"The last drop?"

Juma nodded, as Golo secured the bottle; he was still thirsty.

"Today it's worse," said Juma, looking up at the bright sky. There were no clouds in the sky today.

"No," sighed Golo, shaking his head, "It was the fatty meat I ate for lunch, plus the scorching heat. As you can see, I'm already panting."

As they continued on, the bushes began thinning out; and as if to hasten their pace, a low flying baldheaded vulture swerved past them.

"They got away again," murmured Golo.

He turned his gaze to the vulture that lingeredmid-air. As it descended once again, Golo stopped and waited for Juma, who was a couple steps behind.

"What do you think?"

Juma acknowledged, wiping the sweat that dripped along his forehead.

"They're gone, and it's unlikely that we'll catch them."

"Bastards," hissed Golo, kicking the dirt road. He dropped to his knees, studying the marks on the dirt with angry eyes; there were three boot marks, one on either side, and the third following closely in an elephant track.

Golo stepped on the footprint that followed the trail; his size ten foot were slightly smaller.

"This one must be size eleven or twelve."

Like a predator whose prey slipped through its claws, Golo, irritated by his failure to apprehend the poachers, wondered whether they somehow knew the operational schedules.

These thoughts ensnared his mind, as he paced on the blood speckled path. He turned to Juma again. "Juma, who do you think is responsible?"

Juma shrugged, defeated.

"Well, anybody could do it."

Golo beckoned Juma, as he continued down the path. They walked with precaution, getting closer with each step, anticipating the dreadful sight of horror that would have befallen the suffering habitat. Up in the sky, more vultures appeared, some circling the sky while others flew to the ground; the early arrivals perched on the trees with their incredible wingspans spread at their sides, cropping up their heads as they guarded what remained of the mighty carrion.

"There." Juma pointed out.

The silhouette of a gigantic head appeared, just ahead.

"They're gone," whispered Golo, as he hurried closer.

Juma however, stopped and readied his rifle. "Just a precaution," he said. Golo did the same, as their steps surged forward, light and daring like the hunter in anticipation, approaching a snare. They crept behind the thick shrubs and silently gazed at the horrific sight before them.

The massive body lay still, emaciated and reduced to a hollow cavern; bony finger-like ribs held to the mid-bones by strings of weak ligaments jutting out from all sides. They have already scooped out the flesh with the head inclining towards the rear. At the base, deep incision on both sides set the head apart from the rest of the body; its ears and long tender trunk torn apart.

The scene was gruesome.

"It's a bull," commented Golo, trying to keep his voice steady, "The tusks must have carried over 400 Kilograms each."

"And good money, too," grimaced Juma.

Golo had discovered many scenes like this; some much worse. And it never got easier.

"One day, I'll catch them."

Panting from the heat, Juma looked on and stood back, hesitating.

"What are you up to, following them again?" he asked, looking over at Golo.

"Yes."

"You must be crazy, Golo, the poachers are already on the other side of the river, and soon it will be dark."

"It's all right, Juma. We still have two more hours before the driver arrives. You can go back to the location where we agreed to meet with him, if you want. I'll check the direction of the trail and catch you on the way."

Juma nodded and turned back; Golo watched him walk away, before continuing.

After a short walk, Golo paused to check the footprints. He swept his gaze over the short grasses. "Oh my God," he murmured to himself. Cow hoofs' marks were visible on the parched ground; they'd swallowed the tracker's footprints.

Leaning against one of the few trees on the path; Golo closed his eyes and wondered about his next move. When he opened it, he noticed the vague, thin smoke not far from where he stood, winding its way out of the bushes. He approached the smoking bushes with caution; he was ready.

***

"Stop, or else I'll shoot!" ordered Golo.

But the guy must have seen him first.

He was running like a gazelle cornered by a hungry lion; he jumped over the shrubs without looking backward. It was too late for the second man. Golo was already standing barely five steps away from him, ready with the gun pointed at the center of the man's stomach.

"Don't shoot me, Mr. Golo, please!" A hoarse, pleading voice instantly cut through the bushes. The man put his hands on his head quickly and surrendered.

Golo arched his brows, putting on a face that showed a mixture of doubt and surprise. With the tip of the gun still covering him, the man stood rooted, his eyes and mouth wide open. After putting the handcuffs on, Golo asked, "Who the hell are you? And how do you know my name?"

The man kept quiet, recovering from the initial shock; the silence prompted Golo to scan him skeptically.

"I worked for Aziz, at the retail shop," confessed the man; barely audible.

"Abdul!" cried Golo, surprised, "You're out of jail already, and doing this now."

"Yes," he replied, casting his head downwards, in shame.

Golo dropped his gaze toward the wrapped bundles on the ground, and the poacher's eyes followed him, roasted antelope meat, half-consumed laid covered by a green branch of shrub. And further ahead, pushed beneath the tree under which the poachers were resting before, was the fresh skin of the dead antelope. The poachers had stuffed the raw meat in the folded antelope skin.

"It's not mine!" cried the man, in panic, "It belonged to the man who fled."

"You will tell that in court," replied Golo, unabashed, "And this belonged to him, too, right?" Golo pointed to the bow and arrows lying on the ground. The arrows were probably poisoned; the tips laced with poison from the tree 'Acokanthera schimperi'.

Careful not to touch the poison, he tied the bow and arrows together, and then instructed the man to carry the rest of the things.

Abdul wobbled along, swerving from one side to another, with both arms stretched out and bent at the elbow.

Golo felt no pity towards him, as they made the journey back.

"Where are your friends?" he asked, poking the man in the belly, with the tip of his gun, "Where did you hide the ivory? You better tell me the truth because I know the hideout."

The poacher kept his head down, his hands trembling.

"Save yourself," advised Golo, not giving up.

"I work with Aziz's people, and they're not my friends."

The man was on the verge of tears, but Golo kept probing.

"If you tell me the truth, I will know, and we might work out something." Golo nodded to the man. "Go ahead." He then added in a whisper. "I can finish you off right now, and nobody would ever know. Save yourself."

The man sighed.

"They disguise themselves as charcoal dealers and bury the ivory in the forest in a heap, covering them with soil; just like the woods used for charcoal burning. Then every Friday evening, they put the ivory in a sack and load it onto the Land Rover, together with sacks of charcoal."

"Can you take me there?"

"Yes, but the poachers guard the place during the day, except between four and five o'clock in the afternoon when they change guards. Only two workers and Aziz knew the place. They keep changing the sites. I happened to know by accident. I overheard the guards discussing the schedules of their work, and then followed them."

Golo didn't want to believe him, he looked at the man again, "Did you tell your friend or anybody else about this?"

"No! Mr. Golo, please! I don't want to go back to jail."

Golo stopped, glaring at the man as he thought it over. It was a risk; that was certain.

But right now, it was the only lead that he had.

"Give me your identity card."

"In the pocket of my shirt," replied the poacher, relieved. He raised his hands, causing the bundles to fall.

"I will get it," scowled Golo.

Golo dipped into his pocket and pulled out three identity cards. He shook his head, as he pocketed them. "So you're also an identity card smuggler. Why do you have three different identity cards with you?"

The man kept his eyes on the ground.

"Okay Abdul," said Golo, recalling the name on the card, "I will keep these until three o'clock on Friday afternoon. Come to WQ gas station, and don't blow it up. Because trust me, if you don't show up, you'd better pray not to be sent to jail."

***

At the station, James Kaya was furious. He had found out from the driver that Golo and Juma went outside the day's schedule. The least he wanted to see was another lousy publicity and negative report on poaching. He kept a tab on the various wildlife activities, and the intelligent unit team was a sore in the rear to deal with; Golo worked in the antipoaching unit.

Golo knocked and pushed the door open. The boss closed the file he was reading and raised his head, summoning Golo to sit. Golo pulled out the wooden chair, next to the door.

"We encountered fresh footprints," announced Golo, "They were heading towards the river. We missed them again."

And with those words, he leaned back into the chair and waited.

"I was concerned that the poachers might overpower you. I don't want to lose any of my officers again," said James, sternly. Golo shifted in his seat, under his boss' stare. "I thought Gotu area was empty."

James then looked to his watch; there was twenty minutes left, until the office closed at five.

"I forwarded your name for the promotion. We're opening a new station in Karra, and it's under our jurisdiction. I'm sure you have read about the station in our annual reports."

Golo confirmed with a nod.

"Yes, I read something about it, the article on cheap meat."

"Yes, the meat comes from wild animals. And don't quote me," the boss lowered his head and whispered. "I heard rumors that at the end of each month, police officers hunt for game meat. I'd love to see them caught red-handed and the information leaked to the press." James closed his eyes, and sighed. "Can you imagine the news, flashed all over the papers with the headline '*Police officers caught feasting on antelope meat?*'"

He let out a guttural laugh, before turning his stern gaze back to Golo.

"Anyway, I want you to take up the position at that place effective from next month. You may go now."

Golo shuffled out of the office; his thoughts on his boss' words.

He had little time left. If he could help solve the problem, he would willingly go there, *but couldn't the transfer wait a bit? What would happen to his lists of suspects?*

As he stepped out of the office and made his way home, the nagging thoughts continued on. *Elephants were scarce in Karra, and ivory poaching was rarely a priority.*

The next day, when Juma and Musa arrived at the office; Golo studied them. But he couldn't see any possible sign that they knew about his promotion. So, with a smug tainted smile, he announced it. "The rumor has it that I got a promotion."

"Congratulations!" cried Juma, as he stood up and shook Golo's hand.

"Wait a minute," questioned Musa, with narrowed eyes, "Is this the transfer to Karra?"

Golo turned.

"Yes, why?"

Both Juma and Musa suddenly burst out laughing. Golo watched confused, as the laughing continued for a while.

Eventually a still smiling Musa, quipped, "That was a real demotion."

Golo raised his eyebrows.

"Demotion?"

"Yes, he's right; that was a demotion," agreed Juma, looking from Musa to Golo, "No one with a balanced state of mind could stay in that place. It's the most desolate and remote place in the country. A vehicle will go to that place only at the end of each month. You shop once, and that's all; so if you want to save money, then that's the right place. Otherwise, money is of little use in that area. The only items overstocked are sugar and tea. It's the last place to live on the face of the earth. When are you going?"

But Golo kept quiet.

"We've been told to take Friday off," Juma said, patting Golo on the back, "I'm sorry for how we kidded you. I didn't mean to annoy you. I know how you feel about poaching, Golo; we've been in this together. Elephants are being killed every day right in front of our eyes, and we can't do anything to stop them. Don't think of the transfer as a demotion. The boss has a lot of good things to say about you, only praises."

Juma paused, and looked down the hall at the boss' closed door.

"This place is more dangerous than Karra," he admitted, as he walked back to his chair, "I'm thinking of changing my profession. The publicity given to poaching could hurt the tourism industry, and the boss wanted a clean report."

"We can't run away from the problem," snapped Golo, finally looking up.

"No, but there are certain things that you have to understand," replied Juma, standing his ground, "Don't you see it? We can't win. Remember, those who are at the forefront in fighting poachers won't live long enough to see the end of poaching. Poachers work with the system and know when to strike."

"Are you on their payroll?" sneered Golo. He knew his words were harsh, but right now he didn't care.

"I wish I were. I would have been better off."

Golo raised his eyebrows.

"Don't give me that kind of look, Golo! I'm not holding a live cobra over your head. Listen, before you joined us, I'm sure you heard about the story. The former boss used to go with us during the field trips. At one time, we confiscated about ten tons of ivory stacked under the wooden frame on the back of a lorry carrying some sand. It was common to see a lorry carrying sand for making bricks. They had a permit ready, nobody doubted it, but the boss got tipped. And guess what happened to the cargo? I still don't know the truth, but the order came from somebody high who ordered the cargo be released from what I heard. After a month, the boss got transferred, and then later, he lost his job."

Juma walked back to him and bent down to meet his gaze.

"I saw your evil, witch hunt list."

"What," replied Golo, surprised, "Who gave you my list?"

Juma looked around the office, before lowering his voice.

"Well, I bumped into it, actually. I went to see the boss, and he wasn't there, but his office was open. There was a newspaper with a catchy headline, so I picked up the paper, and the list was hidden in the center of the pages. I was curious, why does my name appear on that list?"

"It's uncouth to read the confidential material. You behave as if you're one of the poachers."

Juma stood straight, shaking his head.

"Well, if you have proof then you better go ahead."

But Golo remained silent.

***

Golo waited for what seemed to be an hour, pacing the corridor of the shop; there was no sign of Abdul. Finally giving up, he decided to go to the hideout alone.

He grabbed his old bike and rode down the path.

As he neared the hideout, Golo heard the distinct sound of a loud engine. He skirted his bike off the path and hid quickly behind a thick cluster of bushes.

A Land Rover came into view, driving slowly down the rough, dirt path. It stopped before a large tree, and moments later, a Toyota Land Cruiser, pulled out from behind the tree, camouflaged in green twigs and thick branches.

A small group of men jumped out of the vehicle and started removing a pile of leaves scattered in one small area. After digging at it for minutes, they slowly began pulling out piles of tusks; passing it along from one to another, until they secured it in the Land Rover.

Golo crawled closer to the site; there were two people seated in the Land Rover. Aziz's appearance was clear to him, but he wanted to see all their faces. As the others worked, Aziz stepped out of the vehicle and looked on. The other door opened, and out followed Musa, standing beside Aziz.

Golo watched, momentarily shaken.

But there wasn't time, so he stooped forward to get a better view. He pushed aside the twigs ahead, and as he did, his limbs suddenly failed; fear engulfed him and his body, while his mind bogged down incapable of any thoughts.

A startling cruel hoarse voice brought him to his senses, "Turn around slowly with your hands up in the air, or else you'll be dead!"

Golo couldn't believe it, when he saw Abdul pointing a revolver directly at his head. Golo tried to speak but could not form any words. With handcuffs on, Abdul dragged him to the spot where the rest of the poachers were waiting.

Golo saw double images of wild, bloody eyes; five pairs all tearing him apart. Aziz and Musa stepped aside for consultations. The order was clear. "Eliminate Golo and two poachers."

Musa protested. "I understand Golo, but why the two poachers?"

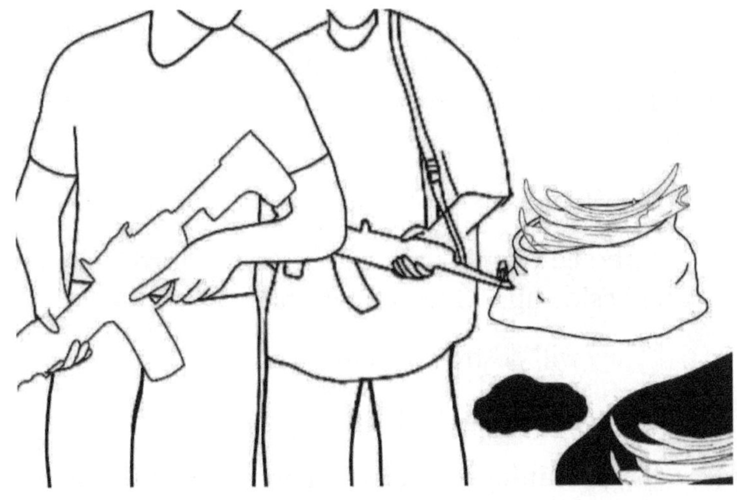

"We no longer have any use for them; those two double-crossed me and they know too much," answered Aziz, emotionless, "I want a clean job, no trace of their bodies. Do it and dump them in the Waso river for the crocs to feast on."

Golo looked on in horror, as he and the other two poachers were dumped into the back of the Land Rover.

Aziz and his team left the site. The silence, like the moment of death, was all around the area; then Golo saw car lights coming towards them. The car slowed down and stopped with the headlights still on. After a few minutes, the vehicle moved slowly, its hooting sound echoing through the bushes. Musa went to the hooting vehicle and came back after what seemed to be another lengthy consultation.

Musa looked at the status of Golo, and the person guarding the prisoners. "Save that for later. They will meet their brutal death, anyway, so don't be too hard on them now."

The guard blindfolded Golo, and then grabbed and threw him. He growled at the sudden pain from the fall. He could hear the soft moans of the other two poachers beside him.

They had transferred them to the other vehicle.

"I thought you were together," whispered Golo, to the others beside him. One of them started moaning.

"They will destroy my family and me."

His other partner hit him.

"Stop whining and act like a man. Whatever happened will happen. My only regret was that I did not take enough." He lamented.

Golo whispered again. "What did you do?"

"Aziz discovered what we did," he said.

"What did you do?"

"I should have taken more. You see, we have been guarding this treasure for over a couple of months, and then we decided to take little by little. I guess we got greedy and looked for a better price. We didn't know that Aziz had a network of buyers. He got suspicious."

As the Land Rover sped down the dusty road, Golo could hear the curses from Musa, for the gullies that crossed his path.

"Oh, my God," exclaimed Musa, "The police have a roadblock ahead, waiting."

Golo remained silent, straining his ears to catch every word and praying that salvation might be upon them.

"Don't stop," ordered Abdul, "Remember, now we're poachers. We have to act like them. I will shoot at them, and you must drive fast."

"No, I can't do that."

"You have to," threatened Abdul, "Or else I will shoot you first."

And that was all Golo heard, as the Land Rover screeched suddenly and began rolling over. As he crashed around the vehicle, Golo slipped into unconsciousness, unaware of what fate had instore for him.

***

Golo slowly came to his senses.

He looked around the small room, wondering why he was lying beside two strangers in the room with a broken limb, and his two companions covered with a bandage on their legs as well.

"Hospital room," he realized.

He saw the blurred outline of police officers in the distance, as his eyelids suddenly became heavy; before he drifted off to sleep, the sound of Juma's voice floated beside him.

"I know him; he's a colleague. Give him time to rest."

Golo woke up the next day with part of his face swollen. Once he was declared fit by the doctor, the officers escorted him out of the clinic.

And standing outside was Juma; waving at him with a big smile.

"You know what?" said Juma, as he walked to him and gave him a big hug, "I have another list. And guess who's at the top? But this time, the promotion is for real!"

Golo laughed and thanked him.

"Did you see this?" Juma flashed the daily paper.

The headline read:

The Chief Game Warden is a trader in the ivory racket.

'Two accidents occurred: a lorry carrying ivory on transit to Nairobi and a donkey cart in a nearby town. The other with a government Land Rover and apolice-mounted roadblock. Both the driver and the unidentified man died on the spot. They recovered five tons of ivory from the Land Rover, and the lorry driver that survived, revealed the names of the owners of the illegal merchandise-James Kaya and Aziz Dawa."

Golo nodded, his face incredibly sad." At least we've stopped some of the poachers," he said.

"Not all of them, I bet," Juma added.

"But we still have a chance," added Golo, holding out his hand to Juma, "Thank you for all your help."

And in the waning twilight outside the game warden's office; they heard the shrill screams of an animal in the distance.

The two friends turned to the sounds and listened; their jobs would never end.

The Village Duksi

The children aged five to twelve, sat huddled together around the bonfire. They had awaken at five that morning to recite the Quran; as the fire kept burning, they continued their recitations. A few others slept while the remainder stood on guard. The fire's flame shot up, casting it's bright light throughout the shelter; a site of learning, where they waited for their teacher Noor Biloi.

Abkul added more firewood, holding on tightly to his *loox* with his other hand, as he pushed more firewood into the blazing flame.

The *loox* was a tablet made out of wood and inscribed with verses of the Quran that the children memorized.

As the children settled around the fire, they all turned their gaze to the hut where their Duksi teacher lived.

"He's coming, quick!" Abkul prodded Hussein, the youngest boy.

Still wearing a sleepy face, Hussein slapped his face lightly before grabbing his loox. The rest of the children rushed to take their place in the simple enclosure, which was similar to the fence people prepared for young calves. They'd erected the shelter and fenced all around with thorn trees, while covering the top with a handmade mat to protect them from the sun's heat.

The children sat in a circle and began the recitations.

But just before he reached the learning enclosure, Noor Biloi slipped over and fell on the side of the path. Abkul and the others giggled, as their teacher rose up and inspected the slippery path that was smeared with mud and filth. Abkul's smile quickly faded, as their teacher glared up at them.

Noor Biloi entered the structure.

Abkul and the rest of the children began every morning the same way; when their teacher entered, they'd sit around the fireplace, and as one child finished the recitation of the verse, they'd move along the circle and begin the other, until all verses of the Quran were completed.

But today, instead of instructing the first chanting; Noor Biloi grabbed a stick and glared down at each of them.

"Who did it?" he demanded.

No reply came.

But this didn't faze their teacher.
"Abkul," whispered Hussein, as he nudged him with his elbow, "Tell him."

But Abkul didn't respond. He saw Hussein shiver out of the corner of his eyes; and knew he was contemplating whether to tell or not. But either way, they both knew that they'd be doomed. If they told their teacher the truth, Wario would be after them.

At least it would be better to receive punishment together as a group, he thought.

When the children missed a recitation or failed to learn verses of the Quran, their teacher would generally blindfold each child with the cloth he used as a turban and deliver instant punishment; the children hated the moment. They never knew which part of the body would receive the blow.

Their teacher, Noor Biloi used three kinds of punishment; slashing while the eyes were blinded with folded cloth, spanking on the bare bottom, or striking on the knuckles.

"Line up!" He commanded.

None of the twelve children wanted to be the firstto receive the punishment; they all fought to be last in the line.

Abkul took the first position in line, and Wario fought his way to occupy the last place. Abkul knew that Wario thought the teacher would be exhausted by the time the blow reached him, and the impact would be less.

He glanced back and saw Hussein, sixth in line; he was trembling.

"I will start with the last person. Wario! Come forward," commanded Noor Biloi, hitting his stick against his hand, "Each of you will receive ten slashes, and then you will walk on your knees up to the gate and back."

"Next!"

But Hussein fell apart when it was his turn. "I know who did it," he shouted.

Wario shivered, looking from Hussein to their teacher.

Noor Biloi nodded, grabbing a fresh stick.

"Wario, you will get twenty strokes and walk with your knees five times."

And with that, he dismissed the rest of the children. While Wario toiled under the cruel sentence, the children continued with the recitation, as expected. After the recitation, Abkul pulled Hussein aside. "Why did you wait until six children got punished? Wario and those other five students will kill you now."

No child was allowed to cry; Noor Biloi had no time for crying babies. A child who sobbed got extra slashes. So no matter how painful it was, they always calmed down after the initial tears.

Their morning recitation ritual was called *Subah*. They sat in a circle and started reciting the verses of the designated chapter. Each child recited a verse of the Quran, then next child in line recited the verse following, and in that order, they would all recite verses after verses of the whole chapters of the Quran and then reviewed all the previously covered verses.

Their teacher, Noor, sat at the center of the circle with a stick in hand, ready to strike. He did not entertain mistakes and careless diversions. If a child made a mistake, he would not be allowed to resume his portion's recitation to memorize and would not proceed further. Thereafter, all twelve children in the Duksi had to return to their memorizations at the level where they stopped the previous day. They had to review with the teacher and were allowed only to move ahead when they passed.

"Go, wash out the *loox*."

Abkul was not alone that day, as other children had forgotten to wash out the previous lessons from the wooden tablet. He lowered it into the water, washed out the material in a specified spot, and then wiped it with a piece of cloth piece. He always used the same tablet for new lessons every time, after committing the materials to memory. Abkul had already made his ink from the charcoal soot and milk, and prepared a thin stick made from a tree branch, to use as a pen. He dipped the flattened tip in the charcoal ink and waited.

"You should be doing that instead of sleeping. Recite! Recite!"

With one strike, Noor Biloi's long thin stick brought the trembling sleepy Hussein to attention. Hussein, the youngest, remained tense. The moment their teacher started the lesson, he panicked. It seemed that things didn't work for him, as it should; he couldn't not help it. His whole body reacted differently whenever the teacher spanked him. Abkul knew that Hussein dreaded the moment when the kids laughed at him, later. He hid it at first, but the kidwho sat next to him brought it to the other's attention. "*Najasa*, you need to make wudu." Hussein peed himself as the teacher repeatedly spanked him on the back. Failing to learn the verses by heart by itself was a terrible mistake, which deserved punishment, but polluting the sacred place with impurity-urine carried a severe punishment that was double or treble more than what he usually got.

The children continued with their recitations. Before they started the individual verses in a group, the initial warming up had long gone, and each of them focused on their respective task. All the children hated Noor Biloi, and his strict disciplinary actions. But no matter how much they complained to their parents, they were always on his side. The elders would emphasize the importance of learning the scripture, no matter how heavy-handed their teacher was. For it was the same way all the children learned when they were kids, they would say. They even had classes sometimes in the evening.

For the most part, life in Barcuma, the remote village in Northern Kenya, remained unchanged, and while people had embraced Islam, in this plain of grassy landscape, they still practiced some elements of traditions. There was little resistance to the new ways of life, and elder Chachu had single-handedly facilitated the religion's spread. It was before the dawn of shifta war. The elders remembered the happy moments back when everyone got swept away in the aura of religious fever. Barcuma village had welcomed the new form of learning and stepped up the competition between villages.

And this was why, no matter how much Abkul and the rest of children complained, the parents never questioned the teacher's handling of the situation. They made it clear that they wanted them to learn the Holy Quran.

For some of them, knowledge was what mattered.It never occurred to them that some children were not learning at all. Few of the children hated this learning method and their cruel teacher, who assumed the omnipotent role of dispatching knowledge through the tip of pain.

It was just after eight o'clock in the morning when the children returned to their respective homes, which was only a short distance from the Duksi compound. Abkul could not help noticing how some of the children reacted to him. It was the same question again and again that he could not answer. They wanted to know why his brother was such a mean and evil person, yet he was supposed to teach them the Quran.

The children knew that Noor Biloi was not Abkul's blood brother, and he was hosted by Abkul's father. As an elder of the village, it was his responsibility. The elders of Barcuma village decided to have Noor Biloi as their children's teacher. Nobody knew who Noor Biloi exactly was. He'd shown up in the village and asked for elder Chachu Dida; and when he met him, he'd asked to teach the Quran to the children.

The encounter may not have been by accident, as some people assumed. Chachu Dida was also a livestock trader, and he'd frequently visit the Wajir district, where this type of Quran learning was actively in progress. He liked what he saw and showed interest in bringing the same kind of knowledge to his village. When Biloi showed up, Chachu knew the time was ripe, and his friend in Wajir must have remembered his desire. He called the elders from all twenty households and convinced them that they had to establish Duksi, a place where the children could learn the Quran.

The only thing they all knew about Biloi was that he did not speak the local language very well. He came from the neighboring District, and Chachu Dida took full responsibility for his care. His family built him a hut and provided him with food-milk every day, and yet Abkul did not see any changes in the way Noor Biloi treated him. The children even gossiped that their cruel teacher would soon get a wife and would speculate whose sister he would likely marry. Abkul hoped that his father would never give Noor Biloi one of his sisters. He could never imagine Noor Biloi as his brother-in-law.

"I said it many times already, he could never be my brother. We are not even from the same tribe; how would you expect us to be brothers?" cried Abkul, as tears gathered in his eyes.

He'd been cornered several times and teased by Wario and his friends. He knew that Wario would later gang up with his friends and beat him, when they took the animals to the pasture. He waited to hear what else they wanted.

"Listen, we're going to do something, and you'd better cooperate. If you ever tell anybody about what we planned, you'll be dead. Tell Hussein that I will get him. Do you remember that pool of water?"

Abkul kept quiet.

He knew the pool all right, but now he'd learned how to swim. But one time before, Wario had pushed him into the water, and only a miracle saved him.

***

Abkul's father, Elder Chachu, took the animals early in the morning to the pastures and drove them back to the village after the sun rose high in the horizon. The lactating cows would rush ahead of other cows to meet with their calves, ready for milking.

Abkul took the last seep of milk and waited. He loathed the impending moment of his daily task; delivering the gourd of milk to Noor Biloi's hut. The role his parents reserved for him, and he hated it.

"Why me all the time?" complained Abkul, "Send Daabo, or Osman. You never send them."

Daabo was his older sister and Osman was his younger brother. His mother just laughed at him.

"You don't like him," she smirked, "I wonder why? He's such a humble man."

"Ya," replied Abkul, with a shrug, "He's evil and mean-spirited like a snake in the grass. He tortures us. In particular, he was hard on me." Tears started dripping along his cheek, and it was then, that his mother studied him closer, and finally noticed the bruises. She hurried over and inspected him.

"Who did this to you?" she exclaimed, "Why did you keep quiet? This was an inhumane act. Did the teacher beat you this much? And all this?"

She turned him around and around. "I will see about this. Now go and deliver the milk."

But Abkul didn't believe that anything could change the situation; his father and the other parents already knew what was going on and did nothing to stop it. So he wondered what more his mother could do to help. Well, he didn't want to lie to his mother, but some of the bruises occurred when Wario and his friends fought with him, and the teacher's beating enlarged the wound.

As usual, Noor Biloi did not talk.

So Abkul put down the gourd of milk and left the hut as quickly as he came. At first, Abkul thought that the teacher hated only his name. But then he realized that Noor Biloi did not like any of the local traditional names, and he regarded them as heathen names; he'd declared that it was sinful to have tribal names. People should get rid of them, he said, and his other actions and attitude confirmed that the teacher punished them as if he had some hidden revenge against them or the community.

Abkul didn't want to believe what the children were saying about the teacher, but he wondered where they heard the story. They narrated that Noor Biloi's parents died during the tribal wars with the neighboring tribe, and he'd left his village for revenge in the name of spreading the religion to heathens. It was evident that the children could invent all sorts of things about Noor Biloi. They'd even said that he wasn't a human, but a beast in the form of a human being. Some said that during the night, he would turn into a lion and roam the jungle; a mythological animal. But all these stories were just the invention of their minds. But even so, Abkul and other children all agreed; there was something about their teacher that seemed odd. Perhaps it was because he didn't know the local Booran dialect very well, and he didn't have many friends. How much do the children know about Noor Biloi? He came from a neighboring tribe, which, in the olden days, was considered an enemy tribe.

Abkul forgot to ask his mother whether what he heard was true.

"How in the world would any father give his daughter to this terrible man?" he lamented, shaking his head, "My father would never do that."

Besides, I don't think any woman with a sane mind would ever stay with him anyway, he murmured to himself.

Later when he returned, his mother remarked. "You see how easy it was to drop the container, and you didn't have to wait."

"Mother! I can't believe what I heard. Is it true that he will live here with us and even get married from around here?" blurted Abkul.

His mother looked at him but said nothing; it was the kind of look he understood. There was something in that look that he understood, and yet he was afraid to interpret it.

"I've heard from you son. Anything is possible. Follow the animals now. Your father is waiting," she finally replied, guiding him with her eyes, "Take care."

And so, with his head hanging, Abkul made his way towards his father.

"Abkul," called his father, when he was finally beside him.

"Father."

"Watch *Koolu*. I didn't like how the cow fed on the grass this morning." When his father grazed the animals very early in the morning and brought them home for milking, he'd usually watched how they behaved closely, "Stay away from the forest near the river. I see some ticks on the animals."

Abkul nodded.

His father always gave him advice like this; the types of pastures to avoid, suitable soils for pastures, names of wild plants and edible fruits, and how to avoid danger in the jungle. And all the other stuff about the jungle, he'd learned from the other kids. Abkul saw the animals from the neighbors' village disappeared ahead of his herd into shrub thicket. His father would soon leave him to continue from thereon. He hesitated, wondering if to tell his father what happened at Duksi, and the teacher. But before he could say anything, his father turned.

"I understand you're very good at getting the Quran memorization right. I heard you are excellent in your recitation and ahead of the rest of the kids. Is he hard on you?"

Abkul looked down. Tears poured from his eyes. *His father must have learned from his mother or the other parents.* "He's very harsh and doesn't tolerate any mistakes. We keep reciting all the time, yet we don't know what those words mean."

His father remained silent as he thought for a moment. Then he patted Abkul gently on the back. So Abkul continued on.

"How long would he stay here?"

"After your training, one of you would take over. Then he may stay or leave."

Abkul kept quiet.

"If there is nothing else, then go in peace."

His father walked away to check on the animals; all of them must leave for pasture. Abkul and the other children drove their animals towards a spot where there was plenty of grasses.

***

At midday, while the animals rested, the boys scouted for berries and roots of edible plants. They shared everything they got, including milk. They watched as the calves approached the cows.

Abkul and Hussein rushed to occupy their spot.

Abkul cupped the palm of his left hand and used his right hand to milk. He swallowed several mouthfuls from his hand. After, Hussein got his chance and was still licking the milk that dripped along his wrist when Wario called them.

"Abkul! I have a job for you." He approached Abkul, who at that moment, was struggling to subdue the defiant calf. He had to hold the hungry calf away from the udder to get some more milk. Hussein moved to another cow in the distance, circling its calf. "Another one is ready!" He called out.

Abkul stopped when he saw Wario holding something in his hands.

"You won't fail us again," huffed Wario, "Make sure it works. You can drop it in the water container, let him swallow it with the water, and it would do the job in the throat or the stomach. This red ant would do the job. Add this as well" Wario picked some berries of *iidi*, a weed species from the family of Solanum nigrum "Crush the seeds from this and drop them in the milk." Abkul continued milking. Wario held in his hand a wrapped piece of cloth.

"What?" Abkul shook his head as if he heard him for the first time.

"You will need to add these in case the first plan failed," continued Wario, rolling his eyes at him, "The solution from the crushed seeds in the milk would work."

Abkul watched as Wario bounced the berries in his hands. "Any fool would know from the smell before he tastes the solution. I won't do it. I tried the other time, and it didn't work. I'm scared of him. Maybe something else. I've decided not to do it alone. We have to do it together. Something that would make him fear us. I am sure we don't want him to die for real. We only wanted to scare him. Or do you want to… "

Abkul would not dare implement this on their teacher. The last time, the plan was for him to drop the scorpion and a poisonous spider on the teacher's clothes while he was out of the hut. But Abkul thought it wasn't right, and although he agreed to carry out the plan, he failed to do it at the last minute, though he kept this to himself. And the scorpion stung him instead. That incident made him believe that their strict teacher might have had supernatural powers, which deflected any misdeeds or evil conducts done against him. Abkul thought the scorpion that stung him indicated a clear warning to any future mischievous acts, and that hidden eyes watched over the holy man. He won't call Noor Biloi a sacred man, because religious people don't inflict pain on others.

Wario designed all sorts of bizarre plans. He wanted to put ants in the drinking milk, scatter thorns along the path of the hut, and release rats into the hut. He even contemplated burning down the teacher's place. However, Wario wanted Abkul to do all this dirty work for him.

But Abkul did not carry out as instructed; he called Hussein aside.

"What do you think about this?" Hussein glanced at the direction where Wario went. Wherever the animals rested, was the spot that Wario liked to lie down and sleep, while the others watched the animals.

"Why do we have to do everything for him? He has to help. He only gives orders," whispered Abkul.

It never occurred to any of the boys that the young Hussein could confront Wario, who was twelve years old with a physical strength twice as much as he was. Like all bullies, Wario thought he had to get his way.

"It's not my turn," shouted Hussein.

"I know, but now it is your turn," replied Wario.

The children took turns to guide the cattle in the right direction; otherwise, all the animals would scatter in different directions, and it'd become difficult to manage. The leading cows had to be directed and restrained. One would need to run ahead and block the animals from going in the wrong direction. And when the lead animals slowed down to graze, other animals would follow.

"We all did our turns, except you." Hussein hollowed.

"Next time he would do it. I decided not to help him with recitation if he either took advantage of you or me. I know he would not like to face Noor Biloi's cane," interjected Abkul.

"What?" cried Hussein, shocked as he wrangled one of the cows, "You want me to obey his commands? Never!"

"No, you don't have to. It's your choice, I guess."

Though Abkul wasn't certain how Wario would take this defiant attitude. The other children heard the shouting and came close to observe what was happening. Abkul looked towards the direction of Hussein and came closer to him. With spear in his hand, Hussein waited. Wario walked to him slowly. The other herd boys moved towards the commotion.

"Don't!" I can use anything if you touch me. I say, don't." Hussein moved aside, ready to throw a spear at Wario if he made an advance towards him. The other children rushed to hold Hussein and took away the spear.

"Look at you. Don't ever play with a spear." Wario grabbed him by the hand. It was so sudden that most of the boys did not know how he did it. Hussein tangled Wario and knocked him down with one blow. He kicked him as he laid on the ground. Wario had no time to respond. He finally got up, but the rest of the children rushed to separate them. Hussein ran, while the other children held Wario and calmed him.

"Where is he?" demanded Wario.

"He's gone," replied Abkul.

***

The next day, when Abkul delivered the milk to Noor Biloi's hut; he was surprised to find him sharpening a knife. Shaken with fright, Abkul stopped. Noor Biloi raised his head and ushered him in with a smile. But as Abkul prepared to move, Noor Biloi raised his hand to stop him.

"Wait. I am not as bad as some of you think I am. I was grateful that your father and your community accepted me in your village. My history may not be relevant for you to know but I consider here my home now. I wanted all of you to learn the Quran. And I learned the same way that I'm teaching you now. I've memorized the whole book, and that's how we spread the word of God. I am here to stay, so tell your little hooligans to stop maneuvering evil plans. I know what some of you have been planning to do all along. One of you told me."

Abkul hesitated. He wondered who could have betrayed them.

"It was not my plan," Abkul shivered, his own words beginning to choke him.

"I don't think so but let the good in you shine. You don't want to disappoint your father."

***

In the next few days, Abkul stayed low as he tried to find out what would happen. He avoided eye contact with Noor Biloi and stopped taking the milk to him; he'd slip away the moment when he was about to be sent. During the lessons, he and Hussein kept to themselves; Hussein had stopped looking after the animals, after the fight with Wario. Wario looked okay and followed them, but Abkul never gave him a chance to speak with him.

The following day was Friday, and it was the only day that they had no recitation in the morning.

Abkul did not look after the animals that dayeither; he and Hussein played the whole day. After the cows came home in the evening, Abkul made the fire at the Duksi compound as usual. It was then that he noticed somebody had been there earlier than his regular time. Some fresh footprints led to the Duksi compound and disturbances on the ground near the enclosure, marked by footprints that appeared to remain in one spot. Abkul glanced towards the edge of the fenced compound. He thought he saw something, but it was dark. He could not figure out what it was. He continued with his fire, and then something caught his eyes. He heard people shouting and running towards the teacher's hut.

The hut was on fire.

"Bring water!"

But Abkul panicked and stood still; he didn't know what to do. Before he knew, an elder grabbed him by the hand and slapped him on the face. "Why'd you do that kind of evil thing?" He slapped him again and again. The hut was almost burnt down by that time, and the desperate struggle to put out the raging fire failed. The villagers converged at the scene. An elder held Abkul by the hand and shouted. " I think this boy set the hut on fire. I saw him in the compound running away."

Abkul could not speak. His father came closer and he saw his mother's eyes streaked with tears. Chachu looked at him once and told the elder to let Abkul go. The people waited.

"Abkul, who did it?"

"I don't know, father. I saw something in the dark when I arrived, but I'm not sure. But I swear, I did not do it."

Chachu told the villagers to disperse; then he told Abkul to leave. Everybody walked back wondering why a kid would do something like that. They murmured and bowed their head down, in shame. Yet, no one noticed the absence of Noor Biloi.

At home, Abkul faced a barrage of questions. He had no choice but to tell his father all that happened the last time.

The next day the elders brought all the children to the meeting and concluded with the prayer. They consulted each other, and Abkul's father agreed to take responsibility. He agreed to pay a bull to compensate for the damages caused by his son.

A week had passed, and there was no teacher; but the children learned as usual. Those children who had completed the Quran helped those who were behind. When they realized Noor Biloi had disappeared and would not be likely to return, the elders met again and appointed Abkul to be in-charge of Duksi. Chachu smiled. "Son, it is your turn now. Teach the children what you have learned."

"Father! Teach them what?" Abkul gapped.

"Quran! Teach them what you know already."

"Father, what happened to Noor Biloi?"

"Nothing. He told me that he would visit the next village. I think he's all right and he'll be back."

"Nothing?" Abkul whispered.

He remembered what he'd heard earlier from one of the boys. They said that Noor Biloi had a habit of appearing and disappearing. And that he'd moved to a village beyond the hills. Some said that he was the one that burnt down the hut, to cover his trace. *Why would he do that?* Abkul pondered.

The children did not miss their teacher, but most of them abhorred what happened to his hut. Some of the children thought only Wario could do something like that, and most of them believed that he did it. Wario boasted to the children that he'd burnt the hut, but he denied it when confronted by elders. He'd even said that he had complicated plans, and since the teacher had disappeared, he would save the idea for future use.

The burning of the teacher's hut was something no villager could ever imagine. It was against the traditional way of solving problems, and some of the villagers believed that an evil curse had befallen the village. People were committing sinful acts, and they feared something terrible would happen to the village. Some other villagers still pointed their fingers at those people who did not accept the spread of the Islamic religion in the area. They believed that new knowledge would erode their tradition and were ready to prevent it. While they exchanged all sorts of rumors and innuendoes, the people didn't even know who committed the crime until weeks later.

Hussein called Abkul aside when they were playing together.

"I have to tell you something," he looked for Wario and the other boys, making sure that they were not close by.

The other children were playing in the ravine.

"It was simply an accident. I wanted to be the first at the Duksi, and when I noticed you didn't come, I went to the teacher's hut to get ambers to make fire, but I spill the hot charcoal near the edge of the hut; I picked all of them up. I never intended to burn the hut. But I was scared and ran," he sobbed into his hands, as his body trembled.

Abkul watched him in disbelief. "Why didn't you tell anybody all this time? And how come I didn't see you?"

"I was frightened. So, I ran and went back to sleep. Besides, Wario admitted that he did it, so I thought it wasn't me."

A long silence engulfed the two friends.

"There are only two choices; either tell the people what happened and free yourself from guilt, or keep quiet because everything is over, and there was no need for a further uproar."

But at that moment, Abkul didn't want to look at him anymore.

Life seemed to return to the little village. Most of the children were about to complete the final chapters of the Quran. Those who completed, celebrated their success by feasting. Many people from the neighboring villages came to Barcuma village to celebrate with them. Abkul's father slaughtered a bull.

Amid all the jostling and excitement, Abkul heard his father called him aside.

"Son," he began. "I knew you did not burn the hut, but why didn't you come forward to let us know who did it? Don't you know that you are as much guilty as Hussein, who committed the act, if you knew and hid the fact from us?"

"I learned about the facts late. But I'm glad that he finally came forward."

Chachu looked at him, with admiration. "I believe you're ready."

He smiled.

***

Abkul had added some fence to the Duksi compound.

It'd took him a while to finish the work that day, and as he prepared to go home, he saw his brother running towards him.

"He's coming back. Dad is going to give him our Daabo. They will marry him," ranted Osman, trying to get out everything at once.

"Wait a minute. Take your time. Who? You mean Noor Biloi?"

Osman nodded.

"Daabo is crying, but mama says it's normal for girls to cry when they hear the good news."

"What news?" asked Abkul, making sure that he'd understood him correctly, "Are you sure?" he added with a forlorn look on his tender face.

Osman just grimaced.

"I can't believe it. He should marry other people's sister, not our Daabo," he murmured to himself.

"I also heard something else. Dad is looking for a girl for you to marry. Guess whose sister?"

"What?"

With a smile, Osman added. "Amina, Hussein's sister. I am sure you won't cry." And with that he ran off.

A Bowl Of Worms

A BOWL OF WORMS

uqa Bariiso, the member of parliament for Isamosa constituency finished his late breakfast and stepped out of the house.

He heard commotions and saw his sister talking with two ladies.

"Boke! Boke! Stop it!" cried Tuqa, coming closer. The two ladies shied away when they saw him. "Hold on, young ladies."

They stopped; Tuqa knew they had not supported him during the previous election. "What good news do you bring us today?"

They answered in unison. "We're just passing through. Your sister accused us of prying into your affairs."

"My dear brother," stated Boke, rolling her eyes at them, "I know these ladies very well, and what they are up to. They are the sources of the rumors circulating in the area about you. Let them leave."

And before Tuqa could hold them farther, they slipped out of the way. Tuqa turned to his sister, wagging his finger at her.

"Look here, Boke, you have to restrain your acid tongue a little. Wait until we're done with the election; people don't want to hear the truth. They would take your words and interpret them differently. What you say matters to them; any word you utter would be taken as mine. And right now, I want you to convince the youth; they're vulnerable and prone to violence."

He recalled the bitter feelings that some people felt during the last elections, and didn't want the same thing to happen, again. *Tuqa did not do anything for the people who elected him for all those years?*

"Boke! Do you think I will lose?"

"No!" she gasped, looking at him in shock, "My dear brother. How can you? Don't be bothered by what they say. And in any case, you have the support from outside forces, which you can always rely on. I've figured out that the registered voters still show our clan's numerical advantage. Even if Bakalcha got all the votes from his clan, he would not win." She came closer to him and whispered, "We'll fix it; Hamisi's on our side. Don't worry." She shrugged and added. "That would leave Juhudi, and of course, the *tiny bugs* he planted."

Tuqa smiled.

The tiny bugs that she referred to were the other two candidates, Jirma and Boru, J & B, as they called themselves.

"Juhudi's just a dreamer. He will not make it, but he will use the *tiny bugs* to split our clans into divisions. That has been his strategy from the beginning," alluded Boke, flipping her headscarf back as she thought hard.

Juhudi had been trying to unseat Tuqa for the last three elections. And even now, he didn't expect any votes from Tuqa's tribe. They had not supported him in the past, but that didn't deter him; he kept going. However, in the last election, he did surprise many people when he came in third out of five candidates.

There were only two candidates from Tuqa's tribe at that time. But now, with four of them vying for votes from one tribe, Juhudi believed that he would make it, with his tribe behind him. He figured that by encouraging J & B to stay in the race, he would advance his chances.

Tuqa and his supporters knew this and saw the danger of this strategy of numbers and the division of votes. With Bakalcha at the forefront, Tuqa focused most of his time on winning over the people who supported Bakalcha. He strategized and was determined to win, regardless of his followers' warnings about the dangerous alliances that Juhudi forged. J & B came from small but united clans, and they voted as a block during the last election. If they did the same this time, that would leave Bakalcha and Tuqa to fight for only their own clans' votes. That was a dangerous gamble for a seasoned politician.

Tuqa knew very well what happened during the last election.

"Boke," said Tuqa, finally breaking the silence, "How are J & B doing?"

"I doubt their combined votes would give them any lead," predicted Boke, with an air of confidence. "Remember the last election? Most of the voters from their clans supported you." She reminded him. "We shall do the same."

"Yaa," Tuqa, sighed thoughtfully.

He paused to reflect on the good times. He had practically no formidable opponents in the past elections. "Things have changed over the years, sister. What exactly are their concerns? I mean those ladies," he asked.

"Just the usual thing. This time they complained about inspector Khamisi, accusing him of voter registration fraud. They said that he disqualified many young people from registering. But they have no basis because he's on our side. So, forget about them."

And with those words, she walked away.

Tuqa pondered over the question; he'd used inspector Khamisi in the past, and he'd done a fantastic job, *but if he refused to register his people, there would be no way they could vote.*

"I'll see the inspector about this," he thought.

Inspector Khamisi had been in the area for the last fifteen years; and he had a bad reputation with the local people. Banditry, wildlife poaching, and livestock theft in the area escalated after he came to Ona town. People believed that the bandits paid him off to look the other way, and as a result, many innocent people became victims. Khamisi also had powerful connections in the government, and Tuqa always used him to get what he wanted. There was no other time than during the election where Khamisi became handy. As a police inspector in the country's remote part, Khamisi set his own rules and bent them according to his needs and whims. He was the law, the judge, and the prosecutor all in one. Tuqa had the power to stop the corruption, but that little favor he sought from Khamisi to win the election made it difficult to change things and do the right thing. So, he got sunk into the habit and looked the other way.

And when the wrong things were not corrected, the right things ceased to exist. The acceptance of false became the norm, and the door of corruption became broader and broader.

Tuqa generally detested this kind of habit, as he knew how corrupt most of the government officials were. The first time he tried politics, Tuqa won many of the people's hearts because he campaigned on issues that mattered to the local people. He convinced them and promised the people that he would provide excellent infrastructure, construct boreholes, provide them with clean drinking water, build hospitals, schools, and eradicate banditry in the area, thus making their lives safer. But that was then, and after 20 years, people did not see any change.

Tuqa had acquired a different kind of taste.

His grip on power led some of his opponents to blame him about the divisive tactics he used to win elections. And it was obvious that he favored his clan over the other tribes. So, he knew he had to retain the glory of power that he'd tasted for the last 20 years at all costs.

All the six candidates (Tuqa, Bakalcha, Jirma, Boru, Amos, and Juhudi) vying for parliamentary seat in Isamosa constituency had started their campaign at the district headquarters, the site of the final tally of all electoral votes. Tuqa read the daily paper and scoffed at the suggestions that Abel Juhudi had turned other tribes around and lured most of them to his side. The article indicated that he had managed to convince Amos Jogoo, the candidate from one of the district's minor tribes, to withdraw. Intrigued, Tuqa read further.

Abel Juhudi aimed to divide the votes; if Tuqa and Bakalcha split their clans' votes and if J & B got some votes from the same tribe, he was sure to eliminate the Bonjo tribe from the equation. Then the other tribes, when combined, would give him the strength he needed. So, Abel concentrated his campaign in urban areas, targeting only the people from different tribes, government workers, and his own tribe, who dominated most of the businesses in the district.

***

A day before Tuqa arrived at Ona, Abel Juhudi called J & B aside.

"I know we're all vying for one seat. But I want to assure you that if I get elected, I will remember you. Ignore what some people are saying about our collaborative venture. It is working, and we have to keep going." Juhudi looked at Boru, while Jirma nodded.

"You know, Abel," said Jirma, "I read the truth of what Plato said about politics." 'In a system in which everyone has a right to rule, all sorts of selfish people who care nothing for the people but are only motivated by their desires, can attain power.'

"What do you mean?" exclaimed Juhudi, shocked, "That's an unfair characterization. I do care. My record is clear, and I've done a lot for the people of our constituency."

"Don't take it personally," replied Jirma, waving him off, "In politics, and we conduct ourselves in strange ways. It's the game, and whatever we do now will be remembered. You know very well that this will be the end of our political career if you get elected because of our collaboration. We shall never face our community again."

Abel Juhudi kept quiet and shook his head. "No, Jirma, we will work something out. You fought for justice, and people will see your honesty. The tradition of clans will die for sure."

"So far, the clan is very much alive. Abel."

Juhudi changed the topic quickly. "Here," he handed each of them some packages.

***

Tuqa arrived in Ona town late that evening; he was somewhat afraid to face the crowd in the daylight, while in the presence of his primary opponent, Bakalcha, who was popular with all the villagers. Word had gone around in the village that Tuqa had planned to meet with elders and that some of his henchmen had already distributed Mirra. The bundles of stimulant were left in preparation for the meetings in the evenings, which usually kept the participants awake long into the night.

The environment was tense; Tuqa could sense it everywhere.

People were no longer whispering; voices were heard from afar, condemning him for his miserable reign. His sins were even depicted in the local songs, and his opponents had distributed CD players. They'd encouraged the people to play the songs in all the shopping centers and the rural areas.

And it was in that moment, he realized how ignorant he had been; all 20 years of his political career would soon be in shambles.

He'd neglected certain things, hoping that the illiterate masses would not know, but things had changed fast. Twenty years was too long to cheat. It appeared to him as if the earth itself was angry with him as well. And for no apparent reason, Tuqa felt sickened with the whole devastating idea. He needed innovative ideas to convince the people for a fifth term.

It was then Tuqa realized, that he'd never invested in effective plans because he occupied most of his time with small talk and his supporters, who never challenged him directly. He rarely sought opinions from anybody else and somehow detested the educated members of the society. He was suspicious and sometimes jealous, of everyone who had ideas for development. He always thought they had ulterior motives; evil plans to topple him and influence people. He watched Bakalcha's actions and was surprised at how he moved into his base quickly.

So Tuqa focused on the next strategy he would use.

***

Bakalcha brought a new brand of politics to the equation.

Yes, it was unfortunate that his opponents focused on the clan factor, but he shrugged them off, saying that he did not choose his parents. Bakalcha often wondered why people concentrated on things they had no power over. So instead, he challenged his opponents to practice what they preached. And on the clan issue, he often told people that he just happened to belong to his tribe because of what his parents gave him and would not take that as privilege either. It was one of those things he didn't have control over, and his goal was, therefore, not to utilize the clan issue. He tried to explain to the people that if they supported one candidate based on the clan factor, it was just like somebody singling out only a father or a mother. A child needed both parents, each of whom contributed fifty percent to the child's making, and yet people seemed to value only the father's side of the clan. Bakalcha was ready to change people's minds on issues of clans. He talked about it at every moment.

No politician liked to be associated with a clan issue, and yet secretly, when they were alone with their clan members, all of them had different agendas.

There was a general assumption that a person born into a clan should automatically support his clan member. Bakalcha had difficulty penetrating these perceptions that people held for so long. And with each election, things got worse; people grouped themselves according to their tribes and voted along the clan lines. Bakalcha was the only person who kept mentioning this problem, and he wanted to do something about it. He laid out his plan and promised to focus on one issue at a time. First, he promised to take care of one stumbling block in his area, the lack of infrastructure.

As the election fever gathered momentum, the supporters of each side intensified their campaigns. They spewed vulgar language and insults against each other. And some even did all sorts of things that they would never imagine doing to their fellow tribesmen, as they damaged each other's reputations. The fever of election had drained the heat of mercy out of every living clan member. They saw everything from their point of view.

It was either Tuqa's or Bakalcha's clan.

And their supporters seemed to disagree on everything. They fought each other more than they opposed any other candidate, outside of their Bonjo tribe. The hostility between the various sectors of the tribe had existed in the past. And yet, the tribe had always kept the balance of power within the clans. These divisive elements were a new influence. It was a borrowed mentality born out of total greed and ignorance of the traditional laws. The Bonjo tribe was known for its unique system in the transfer of power. The clan existed for a purpose and served the whole community, but not to foster an individual's image. No group members would survive on its own. The tradition of kinships, connected through marriages, remained intact. Tuqa's mother was most likely from Bakalcha's clan, and they were considered in-laws by traditional standards. However, during the election, the tribe viewed everything through clan members' eyes and their perspectives.

Everyone seemed to be aware of this quagmire. Even the supporters of other candidates like J & B strongly advocated for the total disassociation with clan politics. They believed that they didn't need a clan to survive, although clan issues had a place in the past when everything a tribal member did was tied closely to the livestock and nomadic ways of life.

Now, there were people who lived in town that did not have animals and some didn't account for their lineage; but when the time of election came, these people maneuvered the campaign and distorted the real issues, to gain the advantage towards the candidates of their choice. These town dwellers had a loose tie to the mainstream. They had no specific ideology or principal to abide by. Whoever provided their immediate needs got their votes; and they were always looking for the maximum benefit. Tribal allegiance mattered to them only during the election, to the extent that, the outcome benefited them.

The history of clans was essential, and Bakalcha didn't want to underscore its significant values. In the olden days, the whole tribe recognized and celebrated the heroic legends of clans' historical events and valor acts, during the intertribal wars. Everything that happened in the tribe was within the context of the clans' cultural values because an individual member who earned recognition relied on his clan member for immediate support. Now, however, this was no longer the case, and Bakalcha tried to teach his supporters to think differently.

***

Abel Juhudi, the only politician from outside the tribe, had studied the politics of the region and the clan issues. He'd attempted to unseat Tuqa three times but failed. But now, he'd gained enough experience and skills from his past failures. And he concluded that if a weaker candidate from Tuqa's Bonjo tribe opposed him, Tuqa would win again, just like he did during the previous elections. With Bakalcha in the race, this time, he knew things would be different. Bakalcha, also from the Bonjo tribe like Tuqa, was a stronger candidate but of another clan. And this turn of event could yield some unexpected luck. He was sure that Bonjo's tribe would likely be divided, and that was the golden opportunity he was going to grasp.

After all, if what Khamisi told him could be ascertained, who knows? The outcome of this election could surprise everybody.

He wetted his lips in excitement.

Abel had no desire to campaign in the areas dominated by Bonjo tribe, as he was certain he wouldn't get even a single vote from them, but he thought he could use his influence and finance to sponsor other candidates who would get some votes from Bonjo tribe. He had secretly financed the candidature of J & B. They would not win the election with Tuqa and Bakalcha in the race, but their few votes would take away some votes from the tribe. It was a smart plan. Abel would exploit their weakness to his advantage. With all the tribe's votes distributed among four people who solely depended on one tribe to win, Abel Juhudi gambled that none of them would be a clear winner in the end. His campaign slogan echoed it all. *"Protect your doors, and I will enter through the windows"* His motto referred to the house as a tribe, and the door as the clan; though some people took this as a mockery. The truth of the matter was that inter-clan rivalry and fighting had paralyzed the area to degenerate it into the least developed part of the country.

***

In the meantime, Tuqa let his mind float with ideas that he had used during the previous election; it was the same views with a different flavor, and it worked in the past, but he also admitted that people needed to use accomplishments as a criterion for success.

He knew what they wanted; and this time, if elected, he promised himself that he would do something different, as he always did.

The people in elder Dima's village gathered once more to discuss the issues about the elections. There were several things to consider, and an already heated debate was going on in one corner of the village. Participation in the election process was not a new phenomenon in the community. However, the candidates' momentum and the involvement by the outside forces had shaped the influence.

Elder Dima would lament.

"Many believed that the outcome, no matter the elders' decisions, threatened the unity of the whole tribe. They mentioned the clan issue as one possible factor in determining the outcome, but in the final analysis, the people felt cheated. Why the sudden resurrection of the clans?" He would ask.

The elders had little control over the changes that happened. Their knowledge of society's cultural values had almost faded away with the advent of religion and the modern ways of living. In analyzing the whole situation, one would conclude that the proponent of this idea stood to gain. They were opportunists diverting the people's minds from the real problems at hand: lack of drinking water and impassable roads. These were the things people wanted to discuss and solve, which were incidentally, the politicians' favored topics before they got elected. But the people were tired of empty words; they needed action, now.

Meanwhile, Tuqa worked hard to boost his faded image, though he still expected to win because he had been in the system, and because of his father, whom people gave enormous respect. He also hoped to exploit the clan's statistical distributions. He argued that he was well known in the area and a favored candidate. Some people would disagree with him. They believed that he was not a popular leader even though they expected him to win the election again.

Few elders met to assess the situations and got disrupted twice; the incident caused a commotion in the village where everything became scrutinized. The elders no longer felt comfortable solving problems through consensus and deliberations. It was only last month during such meetings when the son of elder Dima got contributions towards his education. People did not need to seek any permission to conduct fundraising. Things were changing slowly; with new rules enacted and enforced. The elders were not happy about this change that would require them to get a permit for whatever they wanted to do. People complained about some other archaic colonial regulations, including those which needed them to carry identity cards; the police had used this pretext to arrest innocent people and demanded bribes. Tuqa had not done anything to help remove the repressive rules and some were not happy with him because of it.

In recent years, he'd secretly recruited some of his clans who had crossed over from the neighboring country, and with his friend inspector Khamisi, he'd registered them to vote.

Tuqa camouflaged his weakness by using threats and intimidation, and he knew that things would remain on his side once ignorance, poverty, and antagonism stayed rampant.

"Who could do better than my brother?" exclaimed Boke, boasting to Bakalcha's supporters, "You people forgot the past quickly. My brother will be a minister soon, whether you like it or not. He will win."

No one doubted how the power of outside forces influenced the outcome of elections. Tuqa had used government machinery in the past to elbow his way out and occasionally supported views that were not beneficial to his constituency; the problem of land for grazing and the hostile attitudes of the neighboring tribes who continued to encroach into his constituency remained a real pain for him to settle. He knew he could protect his tribe and their land from being taken away by the neighboring tribes. The boundaries were clear, but he needed some votes, so he allowed the neighboring tribes to settle in one portion of his constituency. However, they kept coming back for more, and now it was too late. They had engulfed his tribe and choked them. Some of his supporters knew the rampant banditry problems in the area resulted from this association and influx of the neighboring tribe into Isamosa district.

And Bakalcha used this issue very well; and people were listening.

Tuqa assessed his strategy again; no matter how the people were attached to the clan issues, when it came to the general affairs of the tribe, they would always come together. And no factor could unite the people more, than the question of land. The people were always asking why no politicians had ever protected their grazing land from the neighboring tribes.

***

"There's nothing wrong with taking back your lands and protecting your property," Bakalcha argued. Bonjo tribe had occupied this land in the past and lived there before the advent of the colonial era. "We should have the full right to decide who should be allowed into our areas."

The next day, two security agents approached Bakalcha and asked him to follow them to the police station.

They read to him the violations he made during his speeches, and, they accused him of inciting the tribe against his neighbors. Bakalcha argued that he did nothing wrong; and just told the truth about his tribe's conditions.

But the security agents didn't care to listen to his arguments; for perhaps, if they were from his tribe, then they would have understood. Instead, they warned him to refrain from using inflammatory words.

Seething, Bakalcha wondered if he should instead speak of the unfair treatment received by the local people, from these government officials. But he knew that they would then accuse him of being a tribalist, inciting, or preaching hatred among tribes.

As he calmed down, he pondered over what the secret agent had told him.

"Don't remind people of the past injuries that they would rather forget. Why not encourage them to live together with other tribes. You always talk about their land. What do they do with empty land without animals?"

It was evident that Tuqa was behind all this fiasco, and he'd used government officials to his advantage. Bakalcha was ready to make the people understand that Tuqa was the real danger to the community's survival.

As he walked into the street, he saw a group of young supporters for his opponent, removing one of his campaign placards. His supporters rushed to the scene and planted another poster with a bold word of his campaign slogan. *Elect Bakalcha and reap the benefit of a lifetime, with success for all.*

Several people approached him.

Bakalcha looked over and noticed that all of them seemed to be from his clan. They were all his dedicated supporters, working hard to make him win this election. They all volunteered without even being asked and conducted door to door campaign for him, yet he did not ask them to be involved. He was amazed by how people took up their roles and worked smoothly; all working towards his election and for his campaign and victory. Most of them even contributed their wealth to the campaign.

Take the case of Haro, one of his chief supporters. He provided Bakalcha the use of his lorry and fed many of his fans at his house. Haro gave out items from his shop at no cost to Bakalcha. They were many other generous supporters who did similar things. In a way, Bakalcha, without knowing, became trapped under the systems of clan influence. He had accused Tuqa of associating only with his clan members who would tell him one-sided information, but Bakalcha failed to notice that his clan members were doing the same thing. They cut him off from the rest of the other members of the tribe. At one time, he told one of his closest friends. "I do understand the relevancy of the tribe in the distant past, but not anymore." Haro nodded and assured Bakalcha that after the election, the tribe will merge again as it had always been. He had seen it through the last four elections and witnessed, brothers, sisters, clan members, and brothers-in-law come together again.

Haro had played his evil part in clan politics. He initially supported Tuqa during the first election, and gave him material support, but when Tuqa started discriminating against him and helped secure loans for his immediate clans, Haro decided to oppose him. The funny part was that people took sides all the time. It was as if they knew what was expected of them right from the start. Politicians knew this trend of events and the actions their supporters took to sustain clan rivalry. Each of them would like to be assured of their clans' votes first, and then when elected, continued to rely on them. People who actively opposed each other remained opposed to each other even after elections were over. Families remained separated because of election disagreement, and in-laws collided over the election issues.

The election frenzy took part in all villages.

The minor candidates had also intensified their campaign; J & B pulled their resources together and campaigned on the same platform. They flatly rejected the idea that Juhudi planted them to spoil the votes for Tuqa and Bakalcha. The fact that they came from smaller clans made them itchy and outspoken; they knew that they would not be elected based on their clans' numerical status, but they made noises anyway.

People who listened to J & B were amazed at their oratory skills. Jirma had prompted them to think and assess their lives, and what they missed because of ineffective leadership. He helped organize a group of elders and took them to other parts of Kenya to see how different places had developed. The eye-opening gesture, as some people would call the event, gained him some respect.

"This is not a friendly crowd," a supporter pointed out.

"I know, but they have to know the truth about why we lagged behind all these years," Jirma assured his loyal supporters.

Jirma walked to some elders gathered under the shade of a shop. Some people decided to disperse when they saw him approach, but he followed them, "brothers, hear my side of the story. This election is about our identity as a tribe. Our two primary opponents have taken us into deep divisions. Our tribe has always acted as one entity but not anymore. We are in new phenomena where the interest of an individual politician dictates how we live our lives. Tuqa and Bakalcha will keep you down for good. Please give me your votes. Check my records of achievement. I have established a scholarship for educational funds for boys and girls. I will consider water, infrastructure, and security problems, and make those issues my priority. I can solve those problems because I know what needs to be done. I am also ready to give out half the amount of my salary to support the community's course if elected, to help with school tuition for needy children," he pleaded, looking around at the crowd, "Give me this chance."

"How much are you paid to divide the community?" someone shouted at him.

But Jirma Qumbi continued as if he hadn't heard what was said. "They tell you lies to divert attention from the real issues. Ask yourselves, after all these years of independence, why don't we have proper telephone systems, roads, and why are there no college in the district or no established livestock market. Why do you transport your animals to Nairobi and end up paying exorbitant prices for transportation, instead of having the animals sold in your town here, keeping the money here to develop our areas? Why? And why? I challenge your current representative Tuqa to tell us, why has he failed to do even those simple basic things for you. Let's face it; each of us has a role to play. If we follow a clan member blindly, it won't help our community to prosper. We must do and follow what is just and good for our community in general. Even if Tuqa did everything for his clans, which I doubt he did, how many people from his clan have benefited? It is probably one or two tycoons, but the rest are still where we were 20 years ago. Don't be fooled by the sheer number of clans. Think and ask yourself what you missed. You can reach Nairobi City within less than five hours from your District Headquarter if you have a good road. You deserve it. It's your rights, and let's fight it together, and we can make it."

The crowd booed him.

Jirma was never alone when he campaigned, so as soon as he stopped talking, Boru Warre picked up where he left.

J & B team campaigned separately, but they often combined their resources and campaigned together. They wanted to clarify that if one of them lost the election, the other got something. Their strategy did not work because most people considered them spoilers, but they fought hard and painted Tuqa and Bakalcha as selfish politicians. They believed that both politicians destroyed the tribe and intensified clans' rivalry. In a tight election, every vote counted, and J & B together could garner about 10 percent of the votes. It was Boru's turn to snap when confronted with a question.

"What makes you think that we are spoiling the votes? We're just trying to prove to you that we're ready to take the mantle of leadership. We are for the community. Give me your votes. If not for me, I guess you know who to elect. My friend," he turned to Jirma. His supporters clapped their hands and encouraged him to speak his mind. Boru continued when the crowd calmed down. "They say we are spoilers. But what are we spoiling? They are telling you that you do not make your decisions. And anybody who disagrees with them is an outcast and considered an enemy of the tribe. You already know what Tuqa did for you all those years, and now Bakalcha wants to take over and continue with the status quo? He will not be any different because he also has his group whose interests he had to serve. We say to hell and down with clans' politics, with one voice for all, let's fight to regain our dignity and rights. This election is about your pride and self-worth. Fight it. Together we can make it." The supporters carried him shoulder high and shouted, singing praise song as they dispersed.

No matter what the opponents said about J & B, the inseparable duo, nobody would count them out yet. They had impacted the way people thought about politics. Few people had started seeing their points of view. The politicians made everybody believe that nothing can be done without them and expected their clan members to act and behave in a certain way. They expected everybody to follow their plans and scorn anyone who had different views. They perpetuated the tension and hatred between people during the election and had divided the community after that.

Some of the young people were starting to question whether the clan was relevant in today's world. Bakalcha understood this aspect of the society but failed to communicate it with the transparency required to win Tuqa's supporters. People took the election issues personally and did not tolerate differences of opinions. A person would turn against you simply if he knew you supported a different candidate. For the next five years, they would remain staunch enemies and continue with these antagonist approaches until the next election.

Just two days before the election, Bakalcha passed through Ona town. He stopped at several shops and campaigned. The issues of unregistered voters pained him, but it was too late to change the situation. His supporters believed that Tuqa instructed inspector Khamisi as usual, but nobody seemed to be sure. Bakalcha was willing to challenge Tuqa on this publicly. The unregistered voters were young people who had come of age and were ready to vote, and they could be Tuqa's voters as well. *Why would he not want them to register and vote?* He pondered over the question. As he walked and mingled with people in the street, Bakalcha found that people remained divided. He had more support from his clan members than fromTuqa's clan. He felt sickened when one of Tuqa's supporters shouted to him, complaining that Bakalcha would deny Tuqa the opportunity to be a minister. But there was no point arguing with a person with that fixedmindset.

They believed that he would be appointed a minister; Tuqa had fed his supporters lies. He told them that he had a guaranteed ministerial position, and the whole tribe would lose this chance if they elected Bakalcha, who had no experience.

The way things turned out, still amused Bakalcha. He still believed he would win this election, but on the other hand, if half of his people were against him, how would he be an effective leader. Besides, his clan's votes alone would not make him a clear winner. It suddenly hit him. He checked his watch. He had to see Haro, his major supporter.

"How shall we turn this kind of thinking to positive. We cannot develop an area when half of the people do not agree on anything. We must learn to respect one another and each other's views. We can disagree on one thing, but it is impossible to disagree with everything simply because we chose different candidates. What about our common goals? What about our common heritage? What about our common cultural values, identity, and language? What about our common needs as human beings? These values are more important than our ego. We should not let this divide and blind us." Bakalcha lamented. His supporters looked at each other. Some of them understood the problem, and he was right in his assessment of the community.

Tuqa's supporters and Tuqa himself knew the problem, *but why didn't anybody stop this deterioration that led to divisions?* Everybody seemed to leave that question alone. They pointed fingers of blame to the opponents. For Tuqa, it was Bakalcha's clan who hated him and planted Bakalcha to topple him. Bakalcha's supporters would also claim that Tuqa and his supporters were out to ruin them and deny their clan members any opportunity. They believed Tuqa's clan wanted to rule all the time and did not accept anybody from a different clan. While everybody seemed to understand the real problem, nobody ever thought the divisions and the breaking up of clans into sub-clans could cost the tribe a seat in the parliament. Bakalcha looked at his supporters and summoned them for a brief meeting.

"I am withdrawing my candidature for the benefit of our tribe. I will not get enough votes to win this election. Therefore, I have decided to step down. We can only win this election if the whole tribe supports one candidate. It is hard for me to face you, but let's look at reality. I do not have a chance." The room remained dead silent. Bakalcha stood for a while and faced sad, gloomy faces. The crowd remained dumbfounded and gaped. They wondered whether they heard him right.

Haro cleared his voice. "Bakalcha, everything you said was right. We cannot go on fighting each other like this. We're all guilty in this, but it would require someone with bravery to admit the mistake. Tuqa would never admit he had any role. Right now, we have to win this election. If you changed the situation after you won the election, you have the power within your reach to do so. Right now, you must win even if it means following a crooked path. It is the game; everybody plays it to win. Let's not cheat ourselves. If Tuqa wins, we will be where we were 20 years ago. I hate to say it, but even if it means destroying the house and building it again, let's do it. There is no time to back off. You forget one important element of our campaign. The people who promised to vote for you will still vote tomorrow. If you withdraw, they will probably not vote at all, and that would be wasted votes, not for you or Tuqa. You took us through all these already. There is no point of return now. Let's elect you first. I will not be in your way, and I will be willing to help you correct past mistakes."

None of his supporters spoke after Haro.

As voting days came closer, many people reported the problems, conflicts, and the crimes' intensity. Bakalcha went to the district headquarters the same day. He knew he had disappointed his closest friends; without them, he would not win. Haro was right. He had to win this election first to change things the way he wanted, but he needed everybody's participation in the community. Empowering the people at the local level and on an individual basis would be his priority.

The final week was tense.

Bakalcha's supporters did not allow him to be alone, and his advisers shuttled him from one place to another. He traveled in different cars and slept in different rooms. Tuqa's supporters also had their rumors. They believed Bakalcha had some fanatics in his camp, and they were ready to do anything to win this election. Each group had staged an imaginary enemy. Tuqa even asked the army to be brought to the area. He wanted to impose a curfew, but during the previous election, when he invited the military to the place, the people felt intimidated, and some of them did not vote. Bakalcha opposed the idea and claimed that the purpose was to prevent them from exercising their voting rights and vote for their choices.

The final week was crucial, and each candidate had to encourage his supporters to go to polling stations early and vote. With only one day to go, Bakalcha's supporters watched and took extra precautions. In the past elections, Tuqa's supporters went from door to door and bought voters' cards from Tuqa's opponents and destroyed them.

"Don't leave everything to chances," Haro advised his group.

He sent Bakalcha to the secluded house with his driver. Bakalcha resisted but to no avail. He urged his supporters not to do anything stupid that they would regret later. He had seen how some of his followers reacted and the vigorous campaign they conducted. Some of them were forceful. Tuqa's supporters, on the other hand, enjoyed the advantage of familiarity with the system. They had the support of local government officials. Some of Tuqa's supporters were wild and had committed some crimes and were never apprehended. Some people in the village reported how Tuqa's supporters committed arsenal in the villages that supported Bakalcha. Several staunch supporters of Bakalcha found themselves on the wrong side of the law. One prominent elder who had been in the area throughout his 68 years could not believe when a security officer asked him to produce his birth certificate. They told him that he was not a citizen. *Where would a 68-year-old man get his birth certificate when he had no record?* He had no history of birth in the hospital and probably didn't know his exact birth date. Elder Bagaja's case was just a few examples that Tuqa used as a campaign distraction, but it did not help Bagaja's village. Several times in the past weeks, the bandits raided villages and stole livestock. They knew who was behind the fiasco, but without proof, there was nothing anyone could do. Some supporters or clan members of Tuqa who lived in the same village seemed to know something.

"No! No! Are you sure that elder Bagaja got involved in the act? This is not the news that we would like to hear a day before the election."

"No, Bakalcha, we don't know who committed such heinous crimes. It never happened in our community, before. No matter how divided people were during the elections, our people never killed each other. Killing is alien to our ways of life, and it has never happened. I know whoever did this was not your supporter. I know them. They would never do something like that." Haro concluded.

"Why did they pick on Bagaja?"

"They believe a person from his village killed one of Tuqa's supporters, but they did not have any proof and evidence. They picked him just for the same reason that they have been harassing him all these years. Bagaja sees the wrong things Tuqa did and spoke about them, and it seems people from both clans, respected Bagaja as a wise man from the tribe. Generally, that would be a downfall for Tuqa."

The supporters murmured.

A member of Tuqa's clan was dead. They accused Bakalcha's clan of the crime, and nobody seemed to look for evidence. Everybody assumed that the other clan members did it. *Did the police also buy into the clan mentality?* Bakalcha and his friends thought. They urged the police to find the culprits and bring them to justice. Out of fear, the people in the village stayed indoors. While the police rounded some for questioning, deepening the divisions.

In the meantime, the election was just a day away.

"Are you sure this would work?" Do your boys know the villages?" asked Tuqa.

"Honorable, we know everything. Besides, our friend, the inspector, would do a marvelous job. You will win." You will never receive any single votes from those villages, but we will take care of it! A supporter concluded with a proverb." *Uleen yo waliin falman abbaa gula baati, haayee"*- In a conflicting claim for a walking stick, the stick will return to the owner.

***

Boke cried; the sharp guttural sound from her voice pierced the atmosphere. Everybody turned their heads.

Tuqa and Bakalcha looked at each other.

The elders shook their heads. Elder Haro said it all with a traditional proverb. *Saa abbaan gaaf cabse, ormi ila bassa, jedhaani dhagete? If the owner breaks the cow's horns, a stranger will gouge out its eyes.* He turned to an elder; there was no reply. They'd all walked away.

The children played around, unaware. At the edge of the crowd, a proud Abel Juhudi emerged to proclaim his victory. Indeed, he had entered through the window and into the house that remained intact over the ages and generations. Yes, the door was tightly closed and well protected, but what use has the door if the windows were left wide open and in disarray.

Elder Haro spat and shook his head. The commotion of disbelief engulfed the confused and anxious crowds. One by one, the elders retreated. Elder Haro turned to the elder on his right side. *"Naami aagaachaa hin dhugeefatiin, dhaaichaalle hin dhugeefattu, the person who doesn't take the hints and warnings will not take the message from the beating."*

The elders nodded in silence, and elder Haro turned around and walked home alone. He lowered his head, wondering what would become of the mighty tribe.

CONFUSED

The two brothers looked at each other, without a word, for a long time.

"You did not forget our language?" uttered Zakayo, tilting his head.

"No," answered Ibrahim.

"And you changed your name?"

Zakayo nodded.

"Yes, I have. They call me Zakayo, and I am a Catholic."

"What is that?" asked Ibrahim.

"Later," Zakayo assured him, and told him to sit down first. The brothers hugged each other again, as tears of joy trickled down and covered their faces. Fifteen years had gone by since the last time they saw each other.

A moment of silence engulfed them, as each became submerged in their thoughts.

"Did father and mother believe and die on the same faith?"

Zakayo paused, making sure that he understood Ibrahim's question. "They died before they converted to Christianity, in their original sin and darkness. They were good people, though. So, I believe that they're in heaven. The Lord will have mercy on them."

He crossed himself.

"La Illaha, Illa laa," Ibrahim mumbled between tears. Then the bell rang, and Zakayo looked at his brother.

"I'm going to Church," said Zakayo, standing up, "I'll take you to the priest next time. Now that you've returned, we'll all be together as members of the Catholic faith."

It became clear to Ibrahim that he and his brother had taken a different route.

"La illaha, Illa Iahu, Mohammadu Rasulullah." *There is no God but Allah, Mohammad is the messenger of Allah.* Subhanal-lahi Amma Yushrikoon-Glory to God (High is He) above the partners they attribute (to Him)," Ibrahim recited to himself; it was a verse from the Holy Quran.

"What did you say," inquired Zakayo, turning back.

The brothers looked at each other with unspoken expressions.

"Do you have a mosque in this town?" asked Ibrahim, breaking the silence.

"Yes, I guess so, but one thing I know is that the Maalim in-charge does not act as a religious man. He's more of a politician than a religious man."

"What do you mean?" Ibrahim retorted.

"I'll tell you later; I had to go now."

Ibrahim stood outside the house and observed; he saw many people walking to a big building. His eyes followed his brother, as he walked with his wife and four children, into the building. He waited for a while and then strolled to the house where people were flocking. Ibrahim peeped through the raised window and saw lines of people, men on one side, and women on another.

The preacher was none other than his brother Zakayo.

Zakayo spoke vehemently about the coming of Jesus, and he retold the congregation about the parables of the lost son. Ibrahim listened in amazement; indeed, the world of his brother was strange. He heard everything he said, for Zakayo preached in his own Boorana dialect. Ibrahim was even surprised that his brother could read.

Ibrahim was not the only person who returned from Somalia after the shifta war ended. His return somewhat attracted attention because of his brother, Zakayo. People knew what happened to those who escaped to Somalia. Ibrahim would boast about how he got unique and rewarding experiences that he wanted to share; he believed that it was God's calling that made him return home. *"There was a purpose why he had to return,"* he would comment.

For the last fifteen years, when he was in Somalia, he and some of the people who'd escaped to Somalia were rounded up and taken to a secluded village, where they settled. They'd lost all their animals; either to diseases or theft, and became impoverished, depending on the government's handout.

Ibrahim and his friends hoped to remain in the country only until the end of the war. They planned to return to their homes, but things didn't work that way; the Somalia government intended to settle them in Somalia. So, Ibrahim and his friends embarked on a mission of building that country. Ibrahim quickly learned handy skills like carpentry and at the same time, studied religion. As the years went by, he and his friends learned to filter the truth from the Somali government officials' false stories about Northern Kenya. Ibrahim heard all sorts of information about his homeland. He understood that the Kenyan army had killed everybody in his home, and that those who survived, were converted to a strange religion by force and were replaced by other tribes, from other parts of Kenya. People shared information by word of mouth, and with all those scary stories from his home area, Ibrahim and the rest of his fellow community members accepted whatever false news they got as facts.

So, Ibrahim adjusted; he learned the Somali language, and was ready to participate in his new country's building. He was glad to be alive. But then by accident, he got full information about his family, from a trader who went to Kenya and visited Garba Tulla.

***

Ibrahim walked to the small town located less than a mile from his brother's house. He didn't know much about Marti's other side, where most of the people of Islamic faith lived. Marti had expanded. Ibrahim walked from one shop to another and kept walking. He noticed people had already learned where he came from and who his brother was. He acknowledged their warm greetings with a slight bow of the head and continued.

"Welcome! Brother, I heard about your arrival and I'm pleased to meet you," said Maalim Zaid Bule, as he offered Ibrahim a handshake.

"You mean, you have two mosques here in this town? My brother never mentioned it to me."

"I'm not surprised, brother. You'll learn more about your brother soon. If you want to remain in Islam, get out of that place as soon as possible. Your brother can sell your soul; he'll convert you to Christianity. He has converted half of our people."

Maalim Zaid then invited Ibrahim to his home. They followed a footpath between the shops and entered an L-shaped building through the back side of the house. The building had two entrances. The house walls were newly painted and plastered with a corrugated, red-painted roof. As they approached the compound, kids ran to meet them. "This is Uncle Ibrahim," said Zaid, as he introduced them to Ibrahim. Ibrahim had adjusted to the customary nuances, instead of calling him by his name; the kids had to call him uncle. The close-knit society had a way of diffusing the tensions and quickly develop relationships. Everyone knew his role in the community; even a total stranger had a place.

"The newcomer, "squeaked a little boy, who pointed his fingers towards Ibrahim.

"Everybody knows you, my brother. Consider this your home. You're welcome anytime."

Safiya, Maalim's younger wife, brought them tea with a mandazi. Ibrahim glanced at her and lowered his gaze. He had heard rumors about how she got married. At that time, the whole village talked, and people passed on to each other what happened. One of the first things Ibrahim heard about Zaid was how he got his second wife. The people condemned the religious leader for taking somebody's wife, but it was a false accusation. The woman had divorced her previous husband, and he waited four months before he married. He followed the religious protocol, and yet his opponents twisted the truth to make him look bad.

"Don't believe everything they tell you around here."

Ibrahim looked at him in surprise; he wasn't sure what he meant. The Maalim's speaking manner appeared convincing, and contrary to what Ibrahim heard about the religious activities in the area, not many people embraced Christianity. And as he gathered more information, Ibrahim noticed the bitter tone Maalim used. He condemned the contributions and the work of Christian missionaries in the area. According to him, they had no right to be here in the first place. Ibrahim heard him comment. *"They need to go back to wherever they came from."*

Ibrahim learned about the water project, the health project, and the irrigation project that Christian organizations helped establish in the area, including many schools. And yet, to his surprise, some people did not want to give them any credits for their significant contributions and the development they brought to the area.

"I'm sure they will go back. As you can see, the seeds of their effort are blossoming. The kids they have educated are now taking over, and they will remain here."

It took time before Ibrahim understood what was going on in the area. During the first few weeks of his arrival, he visited the Mosque and attended Friday prayers. He also had several questions for his brother, and Zakayo would willingly answer him what he knew about Christianity, but he had limited knowledge of Islam, to satisfy Ibrahim's persistent curiosity.

***

"Brother, where do you get meat?"

"From the butcher."

"I know," Ibrahim laughed. "From the town's halal meat stores?"

"We get from a Muslim owned butcher, because we don't have any butcher stores around here."

Ibrahim continued to surprise his brother with his knowledge about Jesus in Islam.

"You have Jesus in your book?"

"Yes, our belief in Islam is not complete without believing in Jesus."

"Praise the Lord," Zakayo crossed himself.

"We have exciting stories about Jesus, but we call him Issa and do not attribute divinity to him. For us, he was a Prophet of God. Christians distorted the real role of Jesus, and all Muslims are required to accord the prophet Jesus the same respect they would give to all other prophets."

One of the first things Ibrahim did, was to inquire about places where he could get a handy job. The only place that ever-employed people was the missionary. The mission had on-going construction, and Zakayo had already asked the priest to give his brother a carpentry job. Another elder from his clan also offered him the position of looking after the animals, but Ibrahim declined the job because the payment was extremely low-one cow per year.

By now, Ibrahim understood the role his brother played in the Christian Community. Zakayo had a silent way of giving him some clues, and it happened during the third Sunday after his arrival. The family had porridge for breakfast. Everything around them came to life on Sundays, as people wore their best clothes with an excitement that Ibrahim could not understand. He sat outside the house in the morning sun that day as he planned to walk to the small town after everybody had gone to Church; he turned around at the sound of footsteps.

"We need to get ready." Ibrahim didn't reply to what his brother said until he stressed the word Church again.

"*La illaha Illa lah.* How can I go to Church, brother? I was even thinking of getting all of you out of the Church and onto the right and correct path. I've been praying hard so that God softens your heart towards his straight path. So, how can I follow you?"

Zakayo laughed.

"Oh, my brother, you talk like one of them already. If only you knew what you're missing. I know you've been under a spell for a long time. But now, it's time to come to the truth and light. We're going to church, which will help you see the light."

It was Ibrahim's turn to laugh, but he was still willing to hear his brother's side and reason with him. He never spoke anything negative about Jesus, except for saying that he was a prophet, like the other prophets of God. And whenever he mentioned the name of Jesus, he always added peace be upon him.

"You're coming," concluded Zakayo, crossing his arms as he stared down at Ibrahim, "We've arranged for you to get baptized, as it is the gift of salvation. Remember, the priest gave you a job, too. So, our family should be under one umbrella. Don't you understand?"

"You're asking me to do the impossible, my brother," replied Ibrahim, shaking his head, "I can't change my faith. May Allah's mercy be upon you."

Zakayo did not speak, so Ibrahim got up and walked out.

He passed through the Christian families' small settlement and went to the Mosque where Maalim Zaid and his Muslim members welcomed him. Ibrahim noticed their curiosity and keen interests, especially when he told them that he would not live with his brother because of his faith differences.

"You see, we knew this would happen. That man has ruined our community."

Ibrahim was not sure whether he understood Maalim, "Who ruined our community?" he asked in a surprised tone. The other people with Maalim laughed.

Then one of them answered.

"He does not want to mention your brother by name. We understand that you've started asking a lot of questions. Some people will tell you anything to discredit Maalim or anyone who stands for our religion."

Ibrahim faced him.

"I hear things that I don't want to hear. I'm not saying people are wrong, but it is no use dwelling in the past. We have to move on and lead by example."

"I agree, and you'll have a bigger role to play here with us. We'll fight until we return all those people to where they belong."

The other person laughed again, but Ibrahim, was perplexed by their actions. He understood religion, but some of the acts and suggestions that he heard from the group were contrary to what he believed in.

"If you tell the people about the true religion and they refuse to follow, then you've done your part. You just have to leave them alone, and the Koran is clear about this.

Let's not play the role of God on earth. Who are we to judge? We have to set a good example."

The smiles from Maalim and his followers faded, as they listened to Ibrahim. And Ibrahim had a sad feeling that they'd expected him to agree with them instead of questioning them.

"What role do you want to play?" asked Maalim, somewhat sarcastically.

"I will participate in any area where my assistance is needed. There are still people that lack some of the basic knowledge of Islam."

Ibrahim did not like the way Maalim and his friends looked at him. "Is there something I said?" He turned.

"No! Take your time and start with your own house first." One of them commented. Ibrahim looked up; it didn't take him long to understand what the man meant.

Ibrahim had observed how people did things around there; they did not challenge their leader, but instead, accepted everything as facts, without correcting mistakes. He loathed this kind of life where people who could do things for themselves, played the victims' roles instead, and pretended that they had no control over things. People even distorted God's words, but expected him to accept and follow it, because the religious leader said so. Still, he didn't know much about Christianity that his brother preached.

"You've done your part. Now, let God carry out his plans. You wanted to force them, and Allah never intended us to do that. It is wrong. We must change our approach now," continued Ibrahim, calmly.

They all remained silent at his words.

CONFUSED

***

Over the years, the community of Muslims clung together and remained stable. Maalim and his followers worked hard to stop the spread of Christianity, though some of the methods they used weren't practical. In a society where traditional values are still upheld and practiced, a new approach that attempted to change the way that people lived proved difficult.

All the religious groups, including Christianity, tried to incorporate some aspects of the traditional values and practices, and made them part of their religion. But Ibrahim strongly opposed this kind of method; he criticized Maalim for allowing a mixture of traditional values and religious beliefs. Ibrahim believed that Islamic and traditional practices should not mix; and that people had to follow the right path of Islam.

"There's no middle way. You can't add some cultural rituals to religious practices and call it Islam."

And Ibrahim didn't keep quiet about this; he would speak about it with the congregation of Muslims and gave his opinions wherever possible. Some people admired his innocence and honesty in the way he approached things. But one thing was clear to everybody who listened to him preach; he understood religion and believed in what he taught. He had a unique way of making people understand religion. He used the local examples and dialects to make people understand the truth about the Islamic ways of life. Ibrahim's straight forward approach and clear message contradicted what Maalim preached.

On one particular day, Maalim called Ibrahim aside after he'd released his other friends.

"I know you've been told everything about this place, and our situation is different. We're on the verge of losing our religion. So, our focus now should be to stop the spread of Christianity. You came at the right time, and we need you now. Start with your brothers' group."

Ibrahim listened intently to Maalim's words and waited until the very end to speak.

"Yes," he began, with a calm smile, "I've asked several questions, and sometimes people tell me things without being asked. And from this I've gathered enough information about the situation. Some of the things I hear are not good, but we still have a chance to correct past mistakes. We don't have to do the same thing over and over if it does not work."

But Maalim interrupted him, flailing his arms.

"If you were in the position, of which I am now, you would see everything a little different. There are people who do not want the way that I conducted our affairs, but I will not let them ruin our excellent work."

"You know what," mused Ibrahim, "You don't have to do anything extraordinary to attract people to Islam. You can win people over by how you conduct yourself and follow the instruction in the holy book. We must lead by example. Islam is quite easy to follow. I don't see why we are concerned about losing members."

Maalim squinted his eyes.

"What is your point? We don't fold our hands and wait for people to run over us and destroy our faith!"

"No, brother, that's not the way we should approach the religious matter. Nobody would run away from God. If

Muslims can convert to Christianity, I think those people have never been true Muslims in the first place, so you did not lose them. They were lost already, ignorant of the religion. They lacked an understanding of Islam." He took a deep breath and continued. "I guarantee you, my dear brother, if they only understood Islam correctly, they would never leave." He touched his chest. "It's here. And once it gets here, nothing will remove it. Yes, we have to keep nourishing it by feeding it with sweet knowledge, and then once they observed the five pillars. Your job is done. They will guide it with their lives. Islam is amazingly simple; we are the ones who complicate things and add unnecessary items and make the religion hard to follow." He glanced at the Maalim and continued. "My biggest worry is not about them. I am concerned about the level of profound ignorance that we condone. We need to focus on ourselves and understand religion thoroughly."

Maalim looked at Ibrahim with a weird, blank expression. "You're confused. I don't understand your implication."

Ibrahim continued.

"In short, what I am saying is that only fools will fight over religion."

Maalim turned suddenly to face him, glaring down, and Ibrahim quickly realized that he said a word that might've shocked the religious leader.

"What I meant was that we don't force people to our faith. We can only tell them and convince them to follow the right path. That does not mean that if people persecuted us because of our religion, we wouldn't fight. We must defend and stand for ourselves in every way, but our goal should be peaceful coexistence. Also, we have to create an environment and educate them until they genuinely believe. Then you don't have to worry them losing their faith."

***

Later that day, Ibrahim called Maalim aside. "I have some ideas about what we need to do. Do you still have money for the projects? We need to have social services, health centers, youth programs, educational outreach, and interfaith, in addition to religious expansion."

Maalim shook his head.

"We invested in the livestock market and Islamic schools; occasionally helping people who were in need. But the project ended a couple of years ago, and we're still waiting for the sponsors. We haven't received anything for the last two years," explained Maalim.

Ibrahim wrinkled his forehead, and watched as Maalim's expression became wary.

"Did you hear anything contrary to what I said?" asked Maalim.

"It won't help to go into what people said, but I heard a different story. People accused you of all kinds of things, Maalim, including fraud and smuggling of illegal goods."

"I did a lot, and people were ungrateful," scowled Maalim.

Ibrahim just shrugged; he didn't want to tell him everything that he'd heard.

"Sure, we can't satisfy everybody. So, let's focus more on religious activities. We need to have preachers who understand the religion. This applies to both sides. What we have right now is a group of heretic and zealous people who were out to get the other side in trouble." He nodded to let Maalim know that he still had something to add. "We need to go beyond that and bring people together with wisdom. We have to relax this rigidity and get out of the ignorance that we seem to embrace."

"I am not opposed to the Christian faith, as you seem to suggest," interjected Maalim, "I worked with Inspector of police and the Chief Inspector at the district level who were both Christians."

"I heard a lot about the close business relationship you had with the authorities, and it did not help to improve the image. The divisions and groupings based on religious affiliations still exist. And it will just be a matter of time. We do not want blood on our hands."

"Ibrahim, we have been patient. You don't know about the missionary activities in the area. They want to convert everyone to Christianity, and we must stop them. But don't misinterpret my words. I don't encourage any violence."

Ibrahim had taken it upon himself to do the right thing, and he knew that doing the right thing meant challenging his religious leader.

"Regardless, I think we need to clean our own house first." Ibrahim ascertained. It was hard for him to believe the scandalous activities people attributed to the local leaders, including Maalim.

***

That evening, Ibrahim preached in the village. He chose a familiar topic on the birth of Jesus and explained the divine power that God had granted Jesus. It was the kind of lesson that some of the people in the Christian villages liked to hear, but Ibrahim related it to the Koran like most of his teachings.

He showed them the connections between all prophets from the first to the last. Ibrahim proved both religions could coexist in the same area, side by side. He appealed to preachers from both sides to watch the words they used and avoid distortions.

And as the minutes passed, Ibrahim attracted crowds from both sides; people stood in the open space and listened. The preacher's voice rose high. Here and there, he heard shouts from the crowd disrupting his trends of thoughts, but Ibrahim continued steadfast and focused as usual. He challenged the group to think deeply about their ways of life. For instance, he would pose a statement like this,

"If we all believe that there is only one God, why would one God create many religions? It does not make sense. I would say though, as far as I know, there has never been more than one religion, but throughout the history of religions, people modified, picked, chose, and changed scriptures to suit their conditions."

He moved to the center and looked over at the attentive ears.

"But God's real word does not change. "

Ibrahim swept the flood of sweat from his face with a handkerchief. The preacher had brought a new life to the religious congregations. He did not spare his own fellow Muslims. He had been critical about some of the things his fellow Muslims did because he believed they had no excuse, for they knew better about their religion. Ibrahim's assertion that those who indulged in alcohol drinking and even chewing the Mirra plant's stimulant leaves should not consider themselves as Muslims, stunned the observers, and they considered him extreme.

"What moral justifications do we have for condemning others if we don't correct our faults." He would ask his friends.

*****

Zakayo met with Church elders to discuss the recent clashes between the youths in the village, over the ground that had been in dispute. When the elders sat down, he began to address them. "Our esteemed elders let me get to the point. We're on the verge of spilling blood over this piece of land. I need us to settle this issue peacefully."

"Are you afraid of confronting your brother?" The elders turned to the lone voice at the back of the seat.

Zakayo looked at the young man and continued. "As our proverb says, Namii diiqqaan, haguuma mukha kutuu dubbiile kuta, hin caaqasiina. We cannot allow youth to lead us in this matter. As the saying goes, *the young person is always in hurry and jumps over words as he does over a tree*. We need to address this issue with care. We cannot win this conflict because all of us see things from our point of view. We are not ready to admit the wrong. Let's not allow emotions to take the better of us."

"We have the priest and the law on our side, why do we care. The land is ours, and we cannot have them on our backs. This side of the town belongs to the mission, and we can't allow them to take this land."

The young man's argument persuaded some elders towards his views; one of the elders raised his hand to speak.

"This time, I have to agree with the young man. We should not allow them to have this land. They will build their Mosque on it and take over the whole area."

And within moments, several people began talking at the same time, so Zakayo had to step in and quell the commotion.

"I suggest we sleep on this matter and have another meeting to resolve this issue before it's too late."

And with that, Zakayo adjoined the meeting. He decided to try a different approach with a few selected elders rather than in an open discussion, as well as consulting with some of his clan members.

The next day, however, before he met with his selected elders, the priest summoned Zakayo.

"The elders were not happy with how you handled the situation. You were not decisive and acted impartially. I've already acquired a permit to erect buildings on this ground."

Zakayo always spoke his mind when the situation demanded, and now, alone with the priest, he expressed his concerns about the land. But after their discussion, Zakayo had a feeling that he'd failed out of favor with the priest and wondered why.

***

On the other side of the town, Maalim Zaid and his team met and declared that the land in dispute belonged to a Muslim man who reserved it for the Islamic Center's

94

construction. So they decided to block any development on the ground. But when Ibrahim heard about the disputed land, he thought of using it as a communal land for all. He wanted everyone to have access to it if they preached only religious issues. His idea was to have people get knowledge in at least something. He believed that learning was essential, and he volunteered to hold his meetings there with his group and invited other people from his brother's side to join and listen.

Zakayo had heard about his brother's vigorous activities, but he hadn't talked with him for a while. He'd failed to convince his young brother and felt terrible about it. There was nothing to talk about with him anymore, but at the same time, Zakayo learned his brother had a different approach to religion. He had attracted followers, and people no longer talked about Maalim Zaid. His brother had gained a reputation for being faithful, honest, knowledgeable, truthful, and courageous in his approach to teaching people the right way. Zakayo believed his brother was lost and still vowed to bring him back to the correct religion, but he didn't know how to convince him. He had been thinking of ways to diffuse the situation and make peace with his brother, but they were groups of people from both sides who engaged in violent ways to justify their actions. They believed in force, and almost everybody thought the other group was at fault.

The Christian camp elders wanted Zakayo to acquire the piece of land in dispute, for the Christian organization. They needed to expand and could use that land for social activities. When it came to religion, most people on either side saw things only from their point of view. Zakayo's group had already become impatient with his soft stand against his brother, as some people argued.

"What do you expect me to do with him? Yes, he is my brother, and we just happen to be on a different side," preached Zakayo.

He was trying his hardest to convince his group to be patient.

On the other hand, Ibrahim also saw the need for resolution. He didn't see the need for shedding of blood over a piece of land. Some of his group also accused him of being too soft to stomach any confrontation with his brother.

But he bluffed them off.

They were others who did terrible things behind his back. Maalim Zaid, however, had given him the responsibility to mediate the problem of the disputed land. Up to that time, nobody had tried to investigate the on-going feud between the groups. They did not want to talk about it. Each of them claimed the property as their own and did not like to share. According to Ibrahim, the solution was to turn this property into a community center and build sports activities for youth to serve both sides, and that seemed the only sensible solution. He did not want to get bogged down, with each side pointing fingers of blame at each other. That evening, Ibrahim planned a special meeting with his group and arranged to meet with his brother.

***

"Bring water! Use everything you can!"

The whole area was agitated; people were shouting for help and helping each other extinguish the fire that engulfed the Church's houses. It took a while before the fire was out. People used all the means available to fight the raging fire, but eventually, they managed to put it out.

96

However, the fire had gutted down two huts to ashes, and an older woman got a severe burn on one of her legs.

Everybody in the small town gathered around to witness the destruction. People were asking who could have done something like that. Already each group had accused the other and defended their sides. Ibrahim was among the people who helped to put out the fire, and so was Zakayo.

Most of the people whispered and stared in shocked.

Ibrahim approached his brother slowly. There were many people gathered around Zakayo; they wanted to find out who started the fire, and already, some had fed him with false information. It is as if they already knew who did it. Ibrahim knew his meeting with his brother would not take place, but he still wanted to greet him and condemn the act, at least. The fire was too close to his brother's house.

But everything happened so fast.

He felt the sharp burn of the slap on his face, as he fell forward, towards the ground. The police officers did not waste time; they handcuffed him and dragged him away, pushing him into the Land Rover. There was commotion all over; people were asking what was going on.

The police drove to the station, which was less than ten minutes from the village. Once they stopped, they ordered Ibrahim to dismount, and he obeyed.

"Why do you take me?" he finally asked, although by now he had figured it out.

The two police officers laughed.

"You've caused trouble in the town since you arrived," one of the officers retorted. The other officer gave him a blanket and pushed him into a small cell. Ibrahim did not need to understand what he should do further. He looked around the tiny room and spread the blanket on the cement floor, making it into a bed.

The next day Ibrahim woke up to the reality of his environment; he wanted to go to the bathroom. It was early in the morning, the time he usually conducted his morning prayers. Ibrahim then remembered why they put a pail near his door. He put it upside down and stepped on it to raise himself to the level of the door frame attached to the roof and peeped through; he saw the police officers outside. That day he missed his morning prayer.

"Hi! Pick your trash and dump it into the toilet over there."

The door opened, and a different police officer gave him instructions. "This is your breakfast." He shoved a bowl of mandazi and a thermos of tea into his lap, before shutting the door behind him. Ibrahim tiptoed towards the tiny window and peeped through. On the opposite side of the cell, he heard guards in low voices. They talked about something that he could barely hear. He put his head close to the opening and listened. The voice sounded familiar.

"Hei," the guard looked towards Ibrahim.

"What do you want?"

"Water."

The guard pointed to the kettle placed beside the door.

"I heard the voice like my brother's."

But the guard just laughed, as he shut the door.

Later that day, Ibrahim faced the police constable. They removed his handcuff and allowed him to sit. The police constable and the guard who brought Ibrahim to him conversed in the Kiswahili language. Ibrahim did not understand the language very well, but he picked a few words. At least he heard they mentioned his brother.

"We know what you did since you arrived in Marti. I have the report here, and many people witnessed what happened last night. You're going to sign this document, and then we will send you to Meru town to face charges of arson, a serious crime. You'll be behind bars for a long time."

The guard who understood his language translated. Ibrahim shook his head. The Police constable stood puzzled. People around here obeyed orders.

"Take him back and work on him a bit."

Just before he locked the door, the guard spoke to him in vernacular, trying to convince him to accept the light offer. But Ibrahim still shook his head. The door closed behind him. It was about noon, and the heat of the sun in the tiny room was unbearable.

***

In the meantime, Zakayo was finishing his meeting with the Inspector. He denied all the charges and accusations brought against him. The lists of complaints against him were long, but the Inspector believed Zakayo created the environment that bred the fight and, hence, the hut's burning. "I wasn't even there when the whole thing happened," fumed Zakayo.

"For now, I will give you a warning. Next time it will be different," warned the constable, "Watch out."

Later the priest arrived at the police station.

When he stepped out of the office, Zakayo asked the priest what he did, but the priest kept quiet. "You know he put me in a cell for something else, not for what happened last night. He and I have crossed each other's paths several times."

The priest nodded. "I know, but we have to be friends with law enforcement. He goes to our Church, and he's on our side. Don't be hard on him."

Zakayo had criticized the police Inspector who'd harassed the villagers in the evenings. On several occasions, people complained about police misconduct in the village. Some of them showed indecent behavior, and Zakayo complained to the Inspector and sent a copy of the letter to the district. The incident had infuriated the Inspector and some of the police officers in the area. They vowed to discipline Zakayo.

"Ibrahim had nothing to do with the fire. They framed him, and he's innocent. Will you help him too?"

The priest paused.

"I think his friends have something to do with his case. They wanted him out. You don't know about that?" replied the priest, shaking his head sadly, "Your brother was a pain; he knew too much and was not afraid to expose things. To them, he was a major threat, so Maalim fixed it."

Zakayo knew the priest had close contact with the Inspector and had information not available to most people in the area, so he did not doubt the statement. There was no reason for him to fabricate the story. "I cannot promise positive results, but I'll talk with the Inspector tomorrow." The priest assured him.

Zakayo prepared to leave.

"Remember, this has nothing to do with our side. Maalim has a history of putting away those who disagreed with him. I'm sure he and your brother are not in the same boat." The priest added.

Zakayo hesitated, Ibrahim mentioned the disagreement, but disagreements alone were not enough to put him in jail. He knew he disagreed with his brother all the time, and Ibrahim even humiliated him when he refused to join him. Other people also believed Zakayo himself had something to do with his own brother's problem with the law. The Inspector's accusation implied Zakayo and Ibrahim were behind the incident that happened in the village.

Who would have wanted to put both of us in jail? Zakayo paused in his thoughts, recalling what Ibrahim said about both leaders. "They wanted to keep our people in the dark, keep them illiterate, and make demons out of those who opposed them. They would stop at nothing to keep the status quo."

Zakayo had a lot of thinking to do. He walked back to his house, but instead of taking the narrow path that led to his home, he took the road that diverged to the town. As he walked, he saw some people gathered around the police's Land Rover about to depart for Isiolo. He followed the crowd to the vehicle, but it sped off before he reached it.

"Who are they taking to Isiolo?"

The person he asked looked down, without speaking. And Zakayo had a bad feeling.

"No, they cannot do that," Zakayo muttered to himself. Several people approached him. They spoke words of encouragement, urging him to secure release for his brother. Zakayo knew he would do precisely that, but he had to figure out how and why his brother was captured and beaten in the first place. His brother was innocent; he won't even harm a fly. People had already put him and his brother in a different competing camp and expected him to oppose him because of religion. He would remain his brother with or without faith, yes, he fought him hard, but he would never harm him because of his views. He remembered Ibrahim's favorite statement, "God has plans for everybody," he would say when confronted.

"Hei," Zakayo turned. It was barely a

whisper. "Are you sure about this?" he asked.

The man shook his head and left him in

hurry.

No wonder why, Zakayo thought. Maalim had not said a word about his brother's predicament. All those false accusations, about illegal trophies and illegal arms dealings. The pieces came together. Who else would have coined all of this? Only those who were close to him and worked with him. His mind raced back and forth between the trio: *the police Inspector, the priest, and Maalim. One of them must know the real reason why his brother was in jail.* Zakayo tried to connect some of events that happened in the past.

He heard the priest mentioned some new form of teachings that his brother had introduced in the area. He said his brother was a radical and probably belonged to a group based outside the country. Zakayo had observed his brother; and they were right. He challenged everybody, including the priest, and believed people did not follow the correct religion. When he preached to the Christian group, he talked about Jesus in the Quran eloquently and swayed many people who never thought that the Quran would have any story about Jesus.

Zakayo pondered and shook his head. *He would never hurt anybody. His brother was not a radical!*

"But then, who would gain from that kind of accusation? What about the other serious accusation that his brother was illegally in the country, and yet he was born here in Marti." Zakayo thought again.

Later in the day, Zakayo got assurance from the Chief about the legality of his brother's document. And it was in that moment, that it all came together. Zakayo remembered the simple comment that the local chief made.

"Don't you get it?" he said. "Since your brother came, many Christian families have returned to the Islamic faith. Who would stand to lose more?"

Zakayo weighed the statements. "Why do you people always think that our side causes anything that happens to one of your own?"

The chief laugh.

"What?" Zakayo snapped.

"Nothing," snarled the chief, as he bade him goodbye, "Go in peace."

Zakayo remembered what his father told him before he died. He'd asked him to look after his younger brother. He was going to keep that promise. *I have to get him an attorney.*

THE KITCHEN SOUP

FOOD AID
FOOD AID
FOOD AID
FOOD AID

The children rushed to the door just before the bell rang for lunch. Some of them had already shuffled their feet, ready to dash out, but Bonsa remained in the classroom. He never hurried to get out of the class until everyone had left. The whole area looked like a deserted field. Not a single child remained in the classroom. Everybody had gone to eat, either at home in the nearby villages or at the boarding hostel's dining hall, which was just about a hundred meters away.

Bonsa hesitated at his classroom's door; finally deciding to visit the town. He was starving that day.

Bonsa was not in boarding school; he'd missed the chance and was instead kept on the waiting list. If someone dropped out or left school, he'd get their spot, but no one had dropped out, and for the last two years, he wished somebody would drop dead so that he could take his chance.

None of the children in Bonsa's class ever noticed that he didn't go out for lunch. They didn't know that he had been going without a daily meal for the past two months now. When the children returned after lunch, he was already in the class, and he was the first to arrive in the morning. At times, some of his classmates teased him, wondering whether he slept in the school compound.

At lunchtime, Bonsa usually walked to the nearby town, at his parent's piece of land where they had a traditional hut structure. He'd walked there, sometimes finding his stepmother or somebody from his family there. At times he would see they had cooked some tea or porridge, or ugali with potato stew. Some days, he was lucky, and would get food to eat, but most days he'd go back to the afternoon class with an empty stomach.

"What did you have for lunch?" asked Ishmael, assoon as he spotted Bonsa, "Guess what I ate!"

But Bonsa was not in the mood for Ishmael's constant torture; everyone in class knew that Ishmael was a show-off. He would come after lunch, pushing his hands near his classmates, and asking them to smell it, to guess what food he ate. It was not difficult to get an answer. Everyone knew the type of food people in the area cooked. They enjoyed either chapati with beef stew, plau (a mixture of rice and meat), ugali from maize flour with meat and potato stew. The only distinctive smell was that of curry powder for the flavor and taste.

Bonsa always declined to smell.

He knew the smell of the food from the chief's compound. He'd pass nearby Ishmael's house every day on the way to school and back, so the smell from their kitchen at the edge of the plot was familiar. It had tortured him for a long time. Some days Bonsa even took his time to pass behind the compound to smell the food from Ishmael's home, but when confronted in the class to guess the smell of food, he refused. Bonsa knew one thing, even though his parents came from a poor background, the chief's son ranked at the bottom of his class of forty students. Ishmael was the last in his class.

"Just wash your hands with soap next time. We've had enough of this already." Jillo rebuffed. The children laughed aloud.

Ishmael turned towards Jillo. "I wonder what would happen to you if the kitchen soup dries out," he mocked.

Jillo walked closer towards Ishmael; they both stared at each other. The bell was going to ring soon, and they dared not fight in the class. Mr. Maura's English class was just about to begin. They knew Mr. Maura's strict disciplinary measure. He always carried a cane and whipped them for any slight mistakes, but if any students made the mistake of fighting in the classroom, the punishment would be severe-ten slashes of the cane on the bare bottom and one-week digging the pit latrines.

When the class ended at 3:30, all the students rushed out of the classroom. Bonsa, again, was the last to leave the classroom.

When he walked out, he saw the rest of his classmates scattered in the school compound. Jillo and some of his classmates were walking ahead of him.

"I'll meet with you on the soccer field," said Jillo, stepping back and watching the others continue.

As Bonsa neared him, Jillo turned towards him and held out his hand.

"I've noticed you yawning a lot," pointed out Jillo, giving Bonsa a sweeping gaze, "And you seem to be getting thinner and thinner."

Bonsa kept quiet.

It was difficult for him to disclose his turmoil after the afternoon class, even to his friend. He checked behind, making sure that they were alone before answering.

"I'm okay," lied Bonsa, unable to look his friend in the eye, "I woke up early and didn't get enough sleep."

Luckily Jillo didn't press further. They both walked for a while in silence, until Jillo invited him to his mother's hut. Bonsa accepted.

Bonsa had been to his friend's home before. Jillo had invited him some other times, and he ate food that Jillo's mother brought.

Jillo's mother, Dhaki, worked at the relief food aid store, and she sometimes helped distribute food to the needy children. After the civil war, when most people lost livestock, some Christian organizations established a kitchen soup facility and provided food every day. Dhaki had the privilege of getting enough food for her family; her children were never hungry during all that time of hardships and droughts.

"I thought I saw you around the kitchen soup area with one of those kids scavenging for leftover food," inquired Dhaki, as she greeted them.

"No, it was not me *haato dhaki*" Bonsa avoided eye contact with her. Like all children brought up in his tradition, Bonsa could not call Dhaki by her name. He would either say, mother, aunt or call her after her elder child.

"How are your parents?"

"They're fine."

He knew that she was aware of his father's problems with the army during the war. Like most people in the area, she knew why Salesa, Bonsa's father was detained for years. The government accused him of helping the shifta rebels. He'd gotten out a couple months ago and was finally adjusting.

He'd now disappeared to look for a job elsewhere. Bonsa didn't know what else she wanted to know. He guessed everybody knew about each other in the community. They knew his birth mother died during the civil war, and they probably also knew that he didn't get along with his stepmother.

Bonsa didn't know how long Dhaki had been watching him as he ate. As soon as his friend placed a full plate of rice plau in front of him, Bonsa didn't look anywhere else. His eyes never left the plate of food. Jillo didn't eat much, murmuring that he wasn't hungry. Within a minute, Bonsa had emptied his plate and didn't refuse when Jillo added some more rice.

It was then that Bonsa realized that Dhaki was looking at him from the corner of her eyes. It made him uncomfortable, but at that time, he didn't think that she had any ill feelings towards him. She was always kind and appealing; he'd admired her strength and wondered how she kept her children fed and healthy. He ignored the rumor about how she got the job at the store. They said she befriended a man who was in charge of the establishment and got the job. But Bonsa didn't care about what the people said about her. As a single mother, she had stayed alive and survived the ordeal of the strife and hunger during the later years of the civil war.

Bonsa continued to make frequent visits; Jillo always invited him. At first, after school, but when Bonsa confirmed to him that he did not go for lunch, Jillo invited him over to have lunch with him every day. The first week seemed familiar for Dhaki to accept that extra mouth to feed. She had enough food for her three children, and she also shared with her other relatives. However, Bonsa's frequent visit during the lunch hour somewhat bothered her.

Bonsa noticed Dhaki's face, and he had a strange feeling that she did not want him there. It was the comments she made to him that hurt him. She would ask him when was the last time he ate or sometimes asked him how many plates of food he usually consumes. Bonsa was not afraid to answer her truthfully, but the way she asked him seemed sarcastic. She would say something like, *"Oh boy, do you normally eat this much? Why don't you chew food instead of just swallowing the whole chunk of a spoonful?"*

Life went on for a while, and Bonsa resisted the invitation for lunch, but Jillo would not leave him alone, he considered Bonsa like a brother.

One day after he had lunch with his friend and was about to go back to class, Jillo returned to his mother's hut to get his book. Bonsa was waiting outside. He paused for a while and thought Jillo had taken more time than needed. Bonsa then returned to the hut to check on him. When he entered the hut, he found Jillo eating food. Bonsa held back somewhat surprised, wondering why his friend would eat for the second time. Jillo hurried. His mother held him. "No, finish the food first." She looked crossly at her son and looked at Bonsa. "He will join you. Go!" she commanded.

Jillo detached from his mother and joined Bonsa.

"I didn't want to eat again, but my mother had to force me to eat. This has happened several times. She thinks that I'm not getting enough." He stopped abruptly.

"I do understand," Bonsa said. "Do what your mother says." He hesitated and then added. "I' m grateful for her hospitality, and I don't know how I can repay her."

"You never talked about your mother." Jillo broke the silence after they had come closer to where Bonsa's stepmother lived.

"I don't have anything to talk about and do not remember. My mother died when I was young during the civil war. She died of cholera. I do remember a little, though; many people cried. At that time, I thought she would come back again. I waited for her to come back, but I didn't know why I had such weird thoughts. I now know when people die, they're gone forever."

"No, they're not gone completely. The dead can become ekhera, a form of a spirit, and roam the earth. My mother says that dead people can help you sometimes."

But Bonsa, shook his head, kicking a pebble on the road.

"I don't think so, because every time my stepmother punished me, I asked mom to help me out, and got nothing."

It was awkward, but soon after, they parted and each of them engrossed in thoughts.

"Bonsa! Bonsa! There you are, I've been looking all over for you," cursed Suube, placing her hands on her hips, "Where in the world have you been? Good for nothing, boy!"

"I'm here now," he replied, dipping his head as he walked to the house, "What is it that you wanted?"

"Aren't you going to spend the night at the animal shelter tonight? Today is Friday, you know?" she added.

Bonsa knew the day. Three days of the week (Friday, Saturday, and Sunday), he was supposed to spend the night in the village. Bonsa and his elder brother took turns staying with the animals that were kept with their family friend. He would help to look after the animals during the weekend, send the milk with villagers to his stepmother, and leave Monday early in the morning for his class. During the rainy season, the animals produced enough milk for all of them, but there was no milk during the dry season. They depended on the porridge, and sometimes drank animal blood to survive.

***

When Jillo walked into his house, he came face to face with his furious mother.

"I can't believe that you're so stupid," she scoffed, "Why did you starve yourself? And don't you ever bring that boy from the street to my home again."

"What's wrong, mom? He was not from the street. I'm sure you knew him. He was in my class and is a very bright student. He would never be on the street." He looked into his mother's furious eyes, "There was plenty of food. You even dump or give away the rest at times, and yet, you do not want to help my friend. He was hungry. Very hungry. He never eats lunch. I think there was nothing for him to eat at his home, and he is the only true friend I have. I thought it was okay for him to eat with us here."

Jillo couldn't stop the tears that flowed.

"No, they have animals," replied his mother, unabashed, "I do not want this boy around here. Do you hear what I am saying?"

"Okay, I hear you. It would only be during lunchtime, mom. I swear. Let me share with him my portion. I mean, the food I normally eat, and the food you gave me was more than I could handle. It was enough for both of us, allow me just during lunchtime, please!" He paused. "Bonsa has nothing to eat at lunchtime, but we have plenty of food. Let me, mom," he pleaded.

Dhaki held him by the wrist. "Let me make it clear again. I do not want to feed an extra mouth. No!" She wiggled her fingers.

Jillo knew it was no use to argue with his mother. She always wanted things her way, but he had his plans. He left the hut to play with some boys in the neighborhood. His younger brother joined him, and they played together until his mother came to call them.

For the next couple of weeks, things appeared normal, and Dhaki did not see Bonsa. She was somewhat surprised and wondered how Jillo obeyed her orders. She felt pleased, but at the same time, she thought Jillo was up to something. She knew him. *He must be up to something naughty,* she thought.

One day, at lunchtime, Jillo observed that his mother remained with him and his brother until they finished with lunch. Usually, she would give them food and leave or kept herself busy in the kitchen. Jillo planned with his younger brother or bribed him with candies so that instead of returning the leftover food to his mother, they decided to put it in the plastic or paper bag and save it for Bonsa. Jillo did not know that his mother had discovered the absence of food on their plates from the time she banned Jillo's visitor. She figured it out and coaxed Isaak, Jillo's younger brother, to tell her what happened to the food they left on their plates. At first, Isaak did not want to let the secret out, but his mother would not take no for an answer, so he told her everything they had done for the last couple of weeks. Jillo looked at his mother and then back at his brother and knew what happened.

***

THE KITCHEN SOUP

Mr. Maura, Bonsa's English teacher, came to class early. He heard a commotion, as his house was close to the school compound, and he could see everything that went on around the school compound. His class would start in twenty minutes, but he decided to check what caused the commotion.

"He started it first," said Bonsa.

"No, it was you," replied Ishmael.

"Come to the office, now," barked Mr. Maura.

The office was the next building; and the other children crowded at the door to hear the slash of the cane. They started counting, One! Two! Three! Four! .... Ten! Some quickly counted to ten. They knew Mr. Maura would give ten slashes for fighting in the class. The children then started arguing; some blamed Ishmael for causing the trouble. "He will never show off his smelly hands again," Jillo retorted. "Bonsa did the right thing," another one added. "Wow, where did Bonsa get cow dung?" another boy asked. The children looked at each other. Many of them had already learned how Bonsa got the cow dung that he smeared on Ishmael's hands. Bonsa came to school every morning from his village where his father kept his animals and had decided to punish Ishmael the next time he asked them to smell his hands. Bonsa hid the cow manure he collected in a plastic bag. The action caught everybody by surprise. It was apparent Ishmael did not expect this gross intrusion of unpleasant smell.

The children rushed again to their seats when they saw Ishmael and Bonsa approached the classroom. Bonsa crept with his whole body, almost touching the ground. He took a deep breath after each step, fighting to hold tears. He got 15 slashes, five extra for bringing cow dung into the classroom. Ishmael wobbled almost to the point of crawling. As soon as he reached his desk, the children burst out laughing. Ishmael could not stand straight. He held onto the desk with one hand and pulled up his chair to sit while supporting his weight on his elbow.

He wiped his tears, lowered his whole body to a squatting position, and slowly sat with one side of his butt hanging. He forgot to put a notebook cover in the back of the pants as the children frequently did when called to the office for punishment. In any case, Mr. Maura had discovered the tricks and ordered the culprits to remove the cover. He would generally add an extra slash of cane for what he called "cheating." The students didn't like him much, not only because of this severe and sadistic punishment, but also because of his unpredictable disciplinary actions. For instance, he did not allow them to speak their mother tongue (vernacular) in the school compound. If students talked in the local language, they would receive a punishment that would include digging pit latrines. Ishmael and Bonsa woulddig pit latrines together. They had no choice but to work together now. The children would secretly help them, but Mr. Maura, their teacher, had uncovered that trick as well.

Mr. Maura, also called Englishman by students, arrived at Watto primary school not more than two years ago, but students had already dug four pit latrines. Some students believed that Mr. Maura had become cruel because of what students did to him the first time he had arrived at his class. They said that a student slipped a scorpion into his bag and when Mr. Maura went to the office to get the book he forgot; it was a rude welcome. Mr. Maura left the class shaken when he got stung.

He believed the students had something to do with the scorpion, and because it was a terrible thing to do; he punished the whole class for two weeks. As a newcomer to the area from another part of Kenya, he was not familiar with the deadly crawling creature. Mr. Maura did not quickly forget the ordeal. He was not happy with many things within this place, and he would not tolerate any discomfort in his classroom. As an outsider to this desolate region, he knew how the local people treated him. There was little he could do to manage the outside world, but he was determined to overcome the adversities inside his control zone.

***

Bonsa visited Jillo's home once in a while but not during the lunch hour. At times he would bring them some milk as well. He thought he needed to return the generosity, but he could only get a little milk when he spent the night with the animals, and even that gesture seemed to get him into trouble with his stepmother.

His stepmother discovered that the milk volume had shrunk. So, she asked him what happened and why the animals produced less milk only the days that he was there. And she found out that Bonsa gave out milk to Dhaki. Bonsa knew his family had little to survive on, and the small quantity of milk he gave out was the only food they had. The gourd he brought to his stepmother in the morning held six glasses, and when he gave out two, there was not enough left for tea, porridge, or ugali.

Bonsa continued to give milk out to Dhaki, and felt obligated, although she was not very friendly. He wanted her to like him, but it seemed Dhaki thought only about the food he consumed at her house. Bonsa then decided not to accept any food from her house, but he visited Dhaki's home because of his friend. At his home, Bonsa had more troubles. His stepmother had warned him already. Now there would be no lunch for him any day he brought home less than six glasses of milk. No excuses would convince her, not even when the cows did not produce enough milk. And no matter how much Bonsa tried, she refused to hear his arguments. "Your brother brings six glasses of milk from the same cows. You can do the same," and she would shut him off with those words.

"Bonsa!"

"Yes, mom?"

"I warned you already, that woman does not need any milk from you. She has food, and her children drink milk every day. They have powdered milk from the kitchen soup. Did you know that she engineered the decisions that disqualified us from getting the relief food?" She paused. "She told the one in charge of the relief, her lover, that we had enough cows and removed our name from the waiting list."

She shook her head, angrily, "Yes, we had some cattle, ten cows to be exact, but only three of them produced milk and that wasn't enough to sustain us. We had many cows before the war. She knows we do not have enough."

"It can't be true." Bonsa protested.

"Open your eyes, kid," she replied, rolling her eyes, "I know this is a difficult time for us, and I've not been a real good stepmother, but I know the malicious, evil people who wanted to destroy us." She twisted her mouth with an incredulous look on her face.

Bonsa was not fond of Dhaki either, he'd sensed some dislike from her, but he would do anything for her son, his friend, who helped him when he was in need.

Bonsa was inclined to believe his stepmother this time because he had observed how Dhaki treated him. How could he forget? If not for his friend Jillo, he would never have stepped into her house. He could still remember how he felt when he gave her the little milk he had stolen from his stepmother. Dhaki took the milk from him one day, but as he left, she opened the lid of the gourd slightly, sniffed it, and then dumped it on the ground in front of him. Bonsa thought the milk was fresh and felt terrible to see his gifts wasted. Bonsa was willing to receive punishment for the missing milk to repay his friend's generosity, but it pained him to see how Dhaki returned his favor. Bonsa now understood that Dhaki could be capable of doing what his stepmother said she did.

***

"Have you heard anything about my father?" he asked.

"Not much, but he'll be back. He would never abandon his family. After we lost most of our animals, he vowed to bring us out of this poverty, but getting a job in a strange town will take time. He'll be back, I know he will. You know he wants you to learn, and I hope you won't disappoint him. You're his eyes to the world." She concluded.

Bonsa recalled how his illiterate father encouraged him to learn everything they taught at school. It had been almost a year, and his father had not come back. He didn't know whether he could trust what his stepmother told him about Dhaki's evil deeds with the kitchen soup. His stepmother tended to add flavor to everything she said. He discovered that every time she said something, it turned out to be something else, primarily when it concerned what other people did to her. However, he wondered why she would block them from getting food, which they provided free, and his family needed desperately.

The days when the lorry brought food to the kitchen-soup storage was usually busy. The whole town knew it. Children would surround the truck being unloaded and watch. Bonsa had been a frequent visitor during this time, and some children even missed classes to see the activities around the kitchen soup. Bonsa arrived after his last class when they finished loading the bags of carrots and potatoes. He met the usual boys, who were not from his class. Some were not in school, and few of them were in lower grades. He did not want them to recognize him, so he put on a tattered, oversized shirt wherever he joined them. The children had discovered that when the people unload the sacks of grain, some food dropped on the ground.

"What did you get?" a mean boy called Mammo, who lived near the village around the school, asked Bonsa. "The usual thing, I came late today. You had everything already."

The children helped themselves to the biscuits and some other edible foods. Some rice, sugar, potatoes, and carrots scattered on the ground as the loaders did their shoddy work in a hurry. To his surprise, Bonsa discovered that Mammo shared with him the food he collected. The other kids feared him because he bullied them and stole things from them.

It was during this time of scavenging that Bonsa learned that something had happened to Dhaki. Mammo and the other children in their scavenging group knew Dhaki very well. She did not treat them well either, and refused to let them collect leftovers. She would instead give the leftover food to the dogs. Bonsa knew this already, but the news about her accident prompted him to rush to her home to find out.

Bonsa listened as Mammo narrated to him what happened to Dhaki.

"You should not have done that." He told Mammo.

"It wasn't me," replied Mammo, defensively, "Dhaki mistreated us. She's the only person at the kitchen soup who treats us like dirt."

"What did your friends do?" Bonsa asked eagerly.

"The kids simply poured soapy water on the floor where she worked to make her slip a little." He smiled. "I heard her legs were fine, except for some bruises and a sprained ankle." He added.

"It is not good to harm another human being, you know," Bonsa said to himself.

***

Bonsa stood outside Dhaki's hut.

"Is that you Jillo?"

"No, haato Dhaki," Bonsa replied.

"Auh," Dhaki turned towards the entrance of her hut. "They are never at home to help. Good for nothing, kids. I toiled and brought them up on my own, and yet, they are never at home to help when I need them most." She lamented.

Bonsa continued to visit Dhaki several times after she had the accident. He asked abouther health conditions and even brought her some firewood and water. Though she didn't believe that he could do the things he did. She also wondered whether he asked Mammo, the boy from the scavenging group, to help her. She was surprised when Mammo and his friends brought firewood for her. Not that Dhaki needed their help. She got help from her friends at the kitchen soup. They supplied her with wood for fuel as she usually helped herself to the ones provided at the kitchen soup. But the kids' acts of kindness moved Dhaki. And she felt remorse that her own kids did not meet her expectations.

"What can I do for you, *haato*," Bonsa asked again.

"I am short of sugar. I needed somebody to run an errand for me. Here," she handed Bonsa some money.

***

As Bonsa prepared to leave for the village on Friday evening, Jillo came in panting from the soccer game.

"Bonsa, did you check your name on the admission lists? Those admitted to the boarding school. I heard that my name was on the list. I'm running there to check it for myself now. Come with me! Your name must be there too."

Bonsa quickly glances through the names posted at the door of the headmaster's office. "Look," Jillo nudged Bonsa with his elbow. They looked at each other, wondering why Ishmael needed the boarding school meant for needy children.

"Read further," Jillo urged him.

Bonsa continued and then stopped, making sure that it was his name, and further down the list, Jillo's name appeared.

Tears of joy poured down his cheek. He had no control over it.

"Waaqi iyeesa hin raafu aayee,"

"What?" Bonsa said.

"It was just a traditional saying which you can interpret as. *The God of poor people does not sleep.*"

They moved away from the board to give room for other children.

Bonsa looked towards the direction of the boarding house. At last, he would not be hungry again. He thought.

MIRRA ADDICT

A li Kuno had to wake up before his usual time of 11:00 am; his wife shook him hard and repeatedly nudged him.

"Is the Mirra lorry early today?" It wasn't even noon yet. He looked at his watch with drowsy glances. He still had two more hours until one o'clock when the lorry would arrive. Mirra lorry was not supposed to come until the afternoon, and that was the only time that mattered to him.

"No, It's Kassim," replied his wife, sadly, as she continued shaking him, "I took him to the clinic. He is in the emergency room now."

Ali didn't respond. He turned around on his side and continued with his sleep.

At times Nuria wondered whether Ali even remembered his children. How could he? Ali was never home to see them; he was either asleep in the morning when they left for school or away from home when the children returned from school, and they went to sleep before he came home. When they woke up in the morning for school, he was still asleep. For the last five years, Ali had lived this kind of life. He chewed Mirra with his friends from sunset until dawn, up the whole night. A habit he found difficult to break.

"It's no use. Wait for your Mirra," she sighed.

Mirra, khat, or Jima, was a stimulant derived from the *Catha Edulas* plant, a shrub grown in Meru Region. The trees could grow up to 20 feet, and it's leaves, or young shoots harvested for chewing. Habitual chewers, like Ali, had been conditioned to the time of arrival; they would wait restlessly.

Nuria counted herself lucky when she first got married. For a woman who had never been to school, her marriage to Ali Kuno was all she'd hoped for: He had a local government job, appeared contempt, spent lavishly and afforded a decent lifestyle. But after eight years and four children, her life got stuck where it began. Now she doubted her future with Ali and her children. She feared Ali could lose his job at any time; he should've lost his job a long time ago, and why they hadn't sacked him so far remained a mystery. His position as a tax collector would have made him wealthy beyond imagination if he had saved the side income he got from the trade, but he squandered it on his habit of chewing Mirra. Other people believed he kept his job because of his connections.

***

Nuria faced the irritated nurse at the clinic; she knew what the nurse would say already.

She'd been through this before.

All four of her children had suffered from malnutrition at some point, and she feared the worst. If her third born child contracted tuberculosis, all her children would be in danger.

"Where is your husband?" the nurse asked with a twisted mouth.

The nurse asked the same question every time she visited the clinic, and every time Nuria gave her the same answers; the nurse seemed to enjoy torturing her with questions.

"The children needed protein. Tell that husband of yours to stop making children if he can't provide for them. We can help, you know."

"What do you mean?"

"Help you space them. Or if you think you've had enough…"

"It is not necessary," interjected Nuria.

***

After Nuria left the clinic, the nurse walked over to the clinical officer in charge of the division, Mr. David Mwema. As she took Nuria's file, she commented, "I wonder why people don't plan when they want to have children. They put their immediate pleasure first without considering the painful consequences of bringing children into this troubled world."

Mr. Mwema nodded, looking puzzled as he browsed through the file.

"She's not the only one. The problem's getting worse."

"Look at this woman," the nurse continued, pointing at Nuria's file, "All her children are malnourished, and her husband is a Mirra addict. Instead of putting food on the table, he spends all the money he earns on Mirra. What a cruel way to bring up children. We have to stop this kind of abuse and protect children."

Cecilia, the nurse, was very opinionated on issues that affected the community. She had little influence outside the clinic, and instead tried to advise them on family planning when women brought their children to the clinic. Some men in the town accused her of polluting the minds of women to go astray. They believed that she encouraged women to disobey their husbands.

When women came to the clinic for family planning, Cecilia would become infuriated. *Why don't men come to the clinic to get advice on family planning?* Cecilia would complain. She asked women to bring their husbands when they visited the clinic, but her request had fallen on deaf ears. So, Cecilia decided to instruct women who would listen. She remembered Nuria from her previous visits and scolded her for not taking the pills she gave her.

Cecilia was not sure whether the message got through to the women she advised. The women often accused her of being harsh, but unless she took action, nothing would change. Cecilia had sent Nuria home a couple times in the past to get her husband, and that day as she checked on the women waiting in line, she noticed Nuria again without her husband. She then told Nuria to leave.

Nuria cried. "My child needs help right now. I cannot force my husband to come. You don't understand."

"I do understand," retorted Cecilia, standing firm, "Stop making babies. You don't need any more children."

Nuria picked her child up, and without looking at Cecilia, said. "You don't have children of your own; how could you possibly understand? You will never understand my situation." She then walked out of the clinic, leaving the card on the desk.

"Take your card, Mrs. Kuno! You will need it next time."

"Keep it!"

And Nuria kept going.

"I know you'll be back," whispered Cecilia, shaking her head at Nuria's departing body.

She observed how other women in the line, looked at her in disgust. She knew they talked behind her back, calling her all sorts of names; but after five years of working in the area, she could understand some words in their language. They considered her to be mean-spirited and without remorse for their deplorable conditions, but Cecilia thought people were not taking this disease (Kwashiorkor) seriously.

She openly criticized women who fed porridge and some starchy foods to their children while keeping nutritious food-meat and stew for their husbands. Cecilia was doing her job. Although she also understood the underlying cause of the problem was the historical events of the war and drought, she believed that some people neglected this major health issue. Soon after nomadic people settled in the town, they lacked their traditional diet of milk and meat.

The clinic records indicated that the two most common types of malnutrition observed in the children who attended the clinic were Kwashiorkor and Marasmus. Kwashiorkor developed because of eating a diet deficient in protein. Some mothers fed their children a maize flour porridge, which had plenty of calories but not necessarily enough protein. Lack of protein had slow growth in some children, with an enlarged liver and impaired water balance also associated. Marasmus resulted from a lack of food: starvation.

***

Ali passed by the Mirra kiosk as he usually did after work. He knew that some of the women who sold Mirra didn't tell him how much they traded. The tax he levied on them depended on the amount they sold that day, so they didn't always tell him the truth.

He used his eyes and a surprise intervention to assess the merchandise for what he would charge. It ranged from Kenya Shilling 300 to 500, and the women hated him. Sometimes he didn't give them receipts unless they asked.

Ali always tried not to provide receipts; he would do that later at his own time. How else would he supplement his salary and meet the demands of his addiction? But these days he had to be careful, though. His job also included going to the market and collecting taxes from livestock traders. For sheep and goats, he charged Kenya Shilling 700, and the range for cattle was 950 and up. Just like with Mirra, Ali took every opportunity to conceal the exact amount of tax he collected. He liked the people from rural areas; they never asked for receipts. So, sometimes he would charge them more. He had ugly confrontations with people in the past, especially those who lived in town. They'd started asking questions and was poking around to find out whether his books were in order. Ali had received a warning from some of his friends about the possible audit that he should expect. In his ten years of work, Ali had made many friends as well as enemies. He'd almost gotten fired before, and only survived because of his relative at the county council. The county council required a specific tax levied on some products sold in the open markets, but some people didn't want to pay them. The most troublesome evaders, according to Ali, were the Mirra sellers, who were mostly women.

Dahabo did not go on the trip to get Mirra that day. She and her three partners in the group took turns to get Mirra from Meru farms. After every fifth day, it would be her turn.

When the lorry arrived in Marti after spending a night at Garba Tulla, it was quickly unloaded and then reloaded with goats and sheep. Then the truck, now filled with people, sheep, and goats would leave for Garba Tulla at 3:00 pm from Marti.

Dahabo and other women would travel to Garba Tulla and spend the night there. In the morning, the lorry would leave for the Mirra farms around the Meru area. The people who brought sheep and goats would quickly sell them and buy gunny bags of Mirra and get ready for the four o'clock return trip to Garba Tulla. Then they would spend the night at Garba Tulla again and leave for Marti the next day.

Ali surveyed the lorry as they unloaded the sacks of Mirra. The bundles of tender twigs wrapped in banana leaves looked fresh. Within a few minutes, the women had transported the bags to several town locations where other women distributed the products. The Mirra sellers positioned themselves under the shade of trees and the veranda of shops.

The sellers would receive commissions as little as Kenya Shilling 250 per day, depending on how many Mirra's bundles were sold, but they rarely made enough money. However, it was the only source of income for many, and they didn't mind sitting the whole day to earn their meager daily bread. Their entire life depended on it. These women understood the hardship they faced and had the stamina and tenacity to make the days come to life. They knew selling Mirra would never make them wealthy, but there was no other option.

Mirra's business had captivated women in several towns.

The Mirra sellers, dealers, and owners had a lot in common. They all wanted to make money at the expense of each other. One old woman was fond of commenting, "When poverty is in your face, anything that will give you an edge, a few pennies here and there, even if it means staying the whole day in the sun, is far better than nothing."

Few people realized the social danger of Mirra. Addiction had paralyzed the young and older adults, and yet they were people who depended on the plant for their survival. The income from Mirra had sustained them and their families.

Every time the "Mirra lorry" rolled into Marti, the residents of the town would come to life. People huddled, shouting at the top of their voices, haggling over the bundles of Mirra. Some habitual chewers couldn't wait until the sellers took their stations and spread out their cargoes. Ali had a rough time forcing his way through the crowd. And, as if drained by a power beyond his control; he sprang to action and conducted mental counts on all the cargoes that were unloading.

Dahabo checked on her Mirra. She'd put aside some bundles for her steady customers who would come to her house; some trusted customers like Ali would pay her monthly. Ali would generally come to Dahabo's station when he was about to close for the day. He would then pick his high-quality Mirra bundles at a reduced price and never charged Dahabo the required tax.

There were women who had observed this favor and whispered to each other; and they concluded that Ali had a secret relationship with Dahabo. In a town where everybody knew each other, people observed each other's movements and made their opinions as facts. Ali had long lists of attributes. Dahabo would consider him a generous, considerate, and a faithful customer.

On the other hand, some livestock dealers saw him as a parasite and an addict, who only survived to nourish his habit at their expense. Ali had all those characteristics, but his wife would find it difficult to place him in any category she knew. She agonized and endured the suffering at home that she didn't want to expose to the outside world.

The reality stared at her, in her face; Ali would not function without Mirra. Ali, a well-dressed public figure who spent money lavishly, could never be wrong to the people in the town. They judged him by his physical appearance of clothes and the job. If only he could alter and hide the damage and loss of his teeth caused by Mirra's extensive chewing, a distinguishable mark that deprived him of a smile. He twitched as he recalled what an angry tax evader once called him; the man had called him a toothless dog, and he'd felt offended.

It took a while over the years since his high school days, but slowly the degeneration and loss of his teeth took a toil. The chewing gradually increased, and the heavy use of a pinch of sugar with chewing had done extensive damage. He now had to get distinctive soft leaves of Mirra. His package would be delivered to his house as soon as the lorry arrived. His wife would then put it in a plastic bag and keep the bundle in water to soften it. Then in the evening, she would crush the leaves, adding sugar and butter. The mixture-a thick, paste-like porridge would be ready for him the next day when he was ready to chew. He would then scoop a spoonful on his tongue, and chew until it melted away. Ali chewed Mirra every day, so the portion sent to his wife would be utilized the next day when there would be no fresh Mirra coming to town.

At Dahabo's house, he would have another portion of Mirra bundles waiting. She would also pound the leaves and make it soft for him to chew. After work, he'd pass by her house, and with one or two regular customers, they would sit and munch until the early morning hours.

***

Dahabo had invested heavily in the Mirra business. She had acquired a commercial plot in Isiolo and two in Marti. *Almost two,* she corrected herself.

Dahabo had planned well; she'd invested and diversified the money she got from the Mirra business. How she acquired the initial capital would raise eyebrows. People had speculations, and some people believed that she coaxed a bank manager into giving her a loan and defaulted. Others would say she befriended a wealthy man and got most of the money from him. Still, they were people who suspected that she got involved in illegal wildlife trophy.

But if you asked her, she would tell you that she worked hard for her money and could prove her hard work. Dahabo went through a bitter divorce eight years ago and experienced hardship, without any source of income. Her husband took her two children and wouldn't even allow her to see them. Mirra's business then became handy. She quickly adjusted and perfected her trade. Her closest friends would say, "Forget what people said about her remarkable acumen in business dealings. Or how she charged exorbitant prices. She did what everybody did but knew how to do business, and they should give her credit."

Some people were jealous of her success and angry with her for convincing a few men to sign off their plots as collateral. She did that only when she realized that they couldn't pay her the money they owed. She was in business, and she had to operate.

MIRRA ADDICT

Dahabo had willingly accepted Ali's credit for Mirra. She ordered expensive Mirra for his daily use, and he agreed to put his plot as collateral. Dahabo made him sign a paper with a lawyer, stating that if he failed to pay her all the money he owed, Ali had to forfeit the ownership of his plot at Marti's location and relinquish it to her. People were amazed at how a woman who had never completed a primary school education, could know all the business transaction procedures. She was sure to get Ali's plot anytime, and she thought it was time to let him know about it. Dahabo understood what men needed, and she knew what she wanted from them. Besides her pleasant personality, she had a ferocious appetite for wealth, clothes, jewelry, and perfumes. She was also a very patient woman but handled her finances meticulously.

Some people would say Dahabo had conducted her affairs mysteriously. But only those who knew her well would understand her potential. She could make men surrender to her, and they paid her well for her supportive services. Dahabo had reserved one of her rooms just for entertainment. Some of her customers would find her place more relaxing and pleasurable than the Mirra they chewed. She would fill the room with the seductive smell of incense, and she arranged all the necessary paraphernalia for the occasion. Those who entered the house would rarely part without buying something from her like cigarettes, matches, or soft drinks, and selected customers like Ali would have condensed milk. Mirra laced with butter, music in the background, and special spiced tea with ginger and clover to go along with Mirra, as they luxuriously reclined on sets of pillows in a state of ecstasy. People were eager to gain her favor. At any moment in time during the night, Dahabo would have no less than five habitual Mirra-chewing customers.

***

Ali arrived at Dahabo's house a little earlier than his usual time, so she called him aside.

"It's about your debts," began Dahabo, with a stern gaze, "I've given you plenty of time to clear them. And now, I'm considering taking the plot."

"Come on, Dahabo. You can't do that to me. What would people say? And my family! Where would they stay?" he said, with a mirthful gesture.

"No, I need to have it now. I've waited for too long. You had the money with you every day. As our people would say, *Yo bubbeen dhufte naamu illa uffi qaabaata jeedhani.* When the dusty wind blows towards you, you will cover your eyes." She looked at him seductively.

"I understand. We're friends." He leaned towards her, "Do you know what people think about us? Guess?"

But Dahabo just shrugged.

"I could care less about what people say."

Ali laughed, "They think we are lovers. Anyway, Dahabo, you have been exceptional and allowed me to take Mirra on credits. I know that is not good for your business, but the money I collect every day is not mine."

"You can borrow it to pay me off and then pay them later. I will give you until tomorrow to pay half and then the other half by the end of the month. Bring Kenya Shilling 30,000 tomorrow. I need the money before I leave for the trip. Tomorrow would be my turn to get Mirra." She concluded.

Ali looked at her. He knew she meant what she said. "Okay, tomorrow."

He then returned to the guest room. His other friends had just arrived for the evening. *You will never get the full benefits of Mirra if you chew alone*, Ali would boast. The moment they started chewing, Ali, Molu, and Gutu got the feeling of being possessed. All three friends were habitual chewers. They had developed a dependency but would never admit that Mirra was a drug. The effect induced by Mirra has been compared to those caused by amphetamines or mild cocaine; and all three friends sometimes combined it with other intoxicants as well.

Laced with the mixed aroma of fresh succulent Mirra and banana leaves, the three friends untied their wrapped packages, kept tightly, to retain freshness and moisture. After the first bundle, about a kilo of Mirra, Ali and his friends started heated arguments. Feelings of exaltation, and an atmosphere of joy, accompanied by uncontrollable loquacity, had overtaken them. Ali would dominate the discussions. They talked and talked and touched almost all topics, ranging from what they read in the papers to local gossips. Ali would boast how his mind became sharp whenever he chewed. Other people would argue that the intense activity they felt would only be temporary. They would soon experience lapses into depression, withdrawal, loss of appetite, hypothermia, increased respiration, and sleep deprivation.

The next day Ali brought an envelope with money and handed it to Dahabo. She put in her bag without opening it.

***

"I can't believe she said my children had Kwashiorkor," Ali fumed as he chewed Mirra. His wife's persistent plea about his children's conditions sometimes crossed his mind, but the pleasure he derived for the moment made him forget them quickly.

Ali felt ashamed; he rarely saw his children and when he did see them, he didn't like what he saw. Emaciated bodies and limbs scrawled around him. He accused his wife of not feeding them properly. At one time, he became violent and physical with his wife when she told him that he needed to go with her to the clinic. She had also brought up the rumor that he'd gone with a prostitute in Isiolo. It was the way she said it that angered him. "How do you make a fool of yourself by going with a filthy prostitute and humiliating yourself? I'm sure you heard all that she said about you." He did not want to hear what the prostitute said. He already listened to what other people said behind his back.

The looser couldn't keep her mouth shut, he cursed. The incident recurring in his mind happened in Isiolo during one of his trips.

"It has been four years, and you know we're not living like a married couple." Ali kept silent. This has been going on for a good four years, and no matter how much he tried to avoid the topic, there was no way of him denying it. He had been in denial about his problem and tried to psych himself out, becoming a stranger in his home.

When Ali started chewing Mirra during his secondary school days, he used to get excited. He would suddenly be possessed by a strong desire to see a woman. Things went well at first, but as he made a habit of rushing for excitement at the climax of his intoxication, he realized the desire dissipated as soon as he met with a woman; it embarrassed him, even though he didn't think that it was a big deal. And this embarrassment kept recurring until he decided to stop acting on impulses. He then found himself hallucinating beautiful things that never materialized. When he woke up late in the morning, he didn't want to remember all those beautiful dreams. Nobody else knew his secrets, not even his closest friends. He believed that there are certain things you would never tell other people. But his secrets were out.

Nuria did everything within her means to keep her life secret. She didn't want to admit the impact Mirra had on her husband. Although he would come home to sleep early in the morning, Ali never touched her in four years. He had a significant change in his behavior that she did not understand and avoided contact with her. When he came back from his nightly sojourn, Nuria heard him and attempted to make her presence felt; but as soon as he put his head down, he was gone. Completely asleep. No prodding or pinching would arouse him. *He must have a lover*, she thought.

At first, she suspected Dahabo and even confronted her, but Dahabo denied it and convinced Nuria that she was not interested in any men around there. But it was Dahabo's question that had left Nuria thinking for a long time; she asked Nuria whether Ali had lost his virility because of the Mirra. Before Dahabo asked her this personal question, Nuria never thought Mirra could cause impotence. Then one day, she requested Ali to chew Mirra at home. She told him she wanted to chew Mirra with him at least one day. He reluctantly agreed. Then the moment she waited came. She had her plans. She prepared herself with a romantic perfume from local Qaya. She even did something out of her character. With a seductive smile, she coaxed him into readiness. Nuria would never forget that day when he pushed her away. She felt dejected and humiliated. It was the way he looked at her; contorted and angry. And keeping that murderous look, he turned away and Nuria withdrew. He said he wasn't ready.

In her wildest dream, she never imagined that a man needed to be prepared to be with his wife. It took Nuria more than a year to accept the fact that Mirra might have robbed him of his manhood and sexual intimacy. He'd lost his appetite and drive.

And to her amazement, he didn't want to be naked in her presence. She wondered what had happened. One time when he was deeply asleep, she groomed with her hands and felt it. She then quickly withdrew her hand in shame, wondering why the devil tempted her to check. She was glad he still had his manly thing, though, but it was flaccid and appeared lifeless and exhausted, probably from the years of Mirra damage. Nuria did not know how to handle her situation. The silence was her way of dealing with her life.

So, she concentrated on her children and household chores. But there were times when she couldn't help but crave for comfort; as a woman brought up in a religious family, she knew adultery was unacceptable and against the Islamic faith, so she would never fall for any act of infidelity. Incidentally, Ali was exceptionally good at reminding her of adultery. He often criticized women who indulged in extramarital affairs that, according to him, ruined the family line and heritage.

Ali knew some of the Koran verses and warned her of temptations. Nuria sometimes argued with him, asking why he never practiced what he preached. She knew Ali's chewing habits and suspected of alcohol drinking, which was against Islam's teaching, yet Ali focused mostly on adultery. She wondered whether he suspected anything. Not that she had anything to hide, but people were fond of creating rumors in this town.

There was one time when Nuria innocently entertained the company of a shopkeeper's son, who engaged her with discussions and stories wherever she visited the shop to buy groceries. This close association raised eyebrows.

Until Nuria realized that the shopkeeper's son's affections were beyond casual, friendly talk, and she put a stop to it. Nevertheless, the baseless rumor continued to circulate, and Ali found out.

Nuria still regretted what happened. In a way, she blamed the man for flirting and taking it too far, although she never accepted him as a friend. Nuria was not that kind of woman, but she found the constant rumors too much for her and felt vulnerable after such prolonged abstinence. Ali never showed a happy face at home. She kept hearing what people told her about his good nature and personality. But when she tried to ask him to tell her what was on his mind, Ali snapped, telling her to mind her own business.

On the rare occasions that Ali was at home, he had become a constant pain. He never stopped criticizing her for doing everything wrong, without explaining to her what was wrong.

Nuria conducted her own business as usual and tried not to dwell on her fears. Her primary concern was Ali's health and the well-being of her children.

So, when Ali came home that evening, he found his wife in a sad state of mind.

"What!"

She did not speak. He turned towards the direction that she was looking at. Walking over, he picked the child up. "He did not get medicine?" He asked. After a long silence, she replied.

"They told me that he needed food, not medicine."

"That's nonsense. It was that nurse behind this situation, right?" protested Ali, "And the sick child needed medicine."

Nuria kept quiet.

"I'll go with you to the clinic tomorrow. They have to give the child some treatment."

The next day, as she waited for her turn at the clinic, her mind wondered how he would react when Nurse Cecilia asked him all those questions, she asked her before. Known for saying things straight to the point, the nurse asked propping questions that people usually avoided.

"This child needs your help," Cecilia observed the way Ali folded his facial muscle in indignation, "We have advised your wife already, and still, the child is getting worse."

"Give him some medicine."

"He needs food. Protein! Mr. Kuno," snapped Cecilia, "He doesn't need any other medicine. We called to let you know about the danger he's facing right now."

Ali didn't need any further explanation; the look on her face said it all. So, Ali shot back a malicious look.

"That's all for now. We need him here next month." Cecilia concluded, walking away.

"Take the children to my mother tomorrow. At least they would have some milk to drink. I'm sure the animals have milk now." Ali told his wife, as they walked away from the clinic.

Nuria heard the same statement several times. He had never gone to his village, where his old sickly mother and father stayed. She shot him a glance.

"Don't give me that look" He knew what she would say. "You've stopped supporting them, and now you want to send the children to your parents, who needed your help? How could they provide what you could not offer your children?" Nuria looked at him and shook her head. "After what you did! You have reduced them to poverty, and I don't know what else you're capable of doing."

"Don't bring that up again! The animals would have died of drought anyway. Yes, I sold some animals. I needed the cash." Ali avoided her gaze.

"Face it. Ali," replied Nuria, not backing down, "The only reason you wanted them to go to the village was that you felt bad that they were diagnosed with hunger disease, and it does not look good on you. It is about your image that you're trying to protect."

"Milk is good for them." He tried to conceal his anger.

"There is no hospital there, and I do not want to go to the village." She snapped.

"Don't talk to me like that." He raised his hand and stopped. "You'll see." He fumed. "Go home!"

Nuria glanced at him; she knew he felt ashamed to be seen with his children. When they reached halfway towards their house, Ali left her and walked away to check on the Mirra market, again.

That evening, for the first time in many years, Ali sat with his family long enough to see his children go to bed. He waited for his wife to comment, but she did not speak. She packed her clothes in a suitcase and made everything ready.

***

The journey to the village took about six hours on foot; the children rode on the back of a donkey.

For the next two days, Ali felt the absence of his family. He ate at his relative's house and returned late at night to sleep. A few days later, a lady from his mother's village came with a message from his mother. She approached him while he was checking on the market.

"Son," interrupted the lady; Ali turned abruptly. "Your mother sent me. Your wife ran away."

"What! Where to?"

The old lady shrugged, with a heavy sigh.

"She disappeared two days ago. Some people saw her in Madogashe, and she sent a message saying that she would not go back to you."

Ali stood and looked at the fragile lady for a long time, before hurrying out of the market. By then, the Mirra lorry had arrived, and the town was packed with people shouting. He stood near the truck and watched the people who were disembarking. He knew most of them, and they knew him.

He felt a chilly vibration along his spinal cord when he saw Mustafa, the government auditor.

He slowly slipped away, but it was too late. Somebody shouted his name.

Ali shook hands with Mustafa.

"I will return today," Mustafa announced. "I need all your records. We have two hours to go through some of them together."

Ali froze. He did not expect this sudden inspection. The auditors preferred secrecy, but in the past, he'd gotten wind from his friend in Isiolo. On many occasions, Ali bribed his way out and destroyed some of the records, but Mustafa was tough and strict, and Ali had never had a chance to socialize with him. In any case, his books were messed up. He used all the money he collected, and he didn't have any cash to hand over to Mustafa. Ali had given the last amount of the money he received to Dahabo.

"I need more time." He pleaded with Mustafa. "Here, these are my books. I'll see you before you leave. Give me one week to balance the book."

"When do you learn to separate work from pleasure? I will make my report, and whatever comes after, it has nothing to do with me. Things will be different now. No more favors."

Ali glanced at him once more, as Mustafa started working right away.

Later, Ali called Dahabo aside. "I need the money I gave you. It's urgent. I need it now."

"I don't have that kind of money now," replied Dahabo, shaking her head, "I'm sorry."

Ali stepped back with his eyebrows raised and curved, as the horizontal wrinkles formed across his forehead. He opened and shut his mouth in disbelief. "This is the moment where I needed your help as a friend. I can also get back more money, and you know it. I know how much I owe you, but I just need to borrow this amount for today to balance the book."

Dahabo looked him in the eye. "I've put back the money into the investment and don't have the amount of cash you're asking."

"Can't you get it for me, from your friends?" He pleaded.

"I don't want to get into debt."

Ali stepped out of her house and to the street. He collapsed before he crossed the road.

***

The local people jammed the clinic, wanting to know what happened to Ali. It would be a while before anybody knew what went wrong. His health had deteriorated, and he'd been warned. The medical officer suspected something was wrong with his liver and sent him to the district hospital, an eight-hour drive.

A week later, he left the hospital with a load of worry. The doctor warned him that he would not live long if he continued chewing Mirra and smoking cigarettes. But Ali was more worried about the loss of his job. The news of his loss reached all corners of the district, no job, no land, and no wife. The county council charged him with funds embezzlement, and his court case was set to take place in one week.

People passed him, and some didn't even recognize him. He had become a familiar face. He stood on the corner of a plot where the Mirra women sat waiting for customers. From a distance, he watched. The urge to smoke pressed him. Ali fumbled in his pockets for coins. He counted. It was not even enough to buy one cigarette stick. He then approached a Mirra seller who also sold some individual cigarettes in a packet and chewing tobacco.

"Give me." He handed her twenty shillings. The woman scooped chewing tobacco in a Coca-Cola bottle lid, wrapped in magazine paper, and gave him. Ali snatched the paper and moved aside. He rolled the chewing tobacco in an old newspaper and cut it for one cigarette. He held it in his mouth and lit the end of the folded paper made into a cigarette. He had to use three matchsticks before the smoke engulfed his mouth. After a while, he chewed on edge and kept it in his mouth.

A boy from the neighbor's home came closer to Ali and watched him. "What are you looking at?" Ali snapped.

Ali watched the boy as he ran to the Mirra market corner. People stared at him, and he could hear their murmuring; they were some who even stepped out of the way when they met him.

Ali went to see Dahabo later. Just before he knocked on the door, her maid told him that Dahabo was not in the house, but he was sure that he saw her entering a few minutes ago.

"She no longer gives Mirra on credits," The maid said after Ali turned to leave.

He then went to see Gutu, one of his friends. His mother was at Gutu's house.

"Oh, son, what have you done to yourself?" She wept. Ali watched, calm, his eyes unblinking. She wiped her tears. "You have to come home with me. The children will be fine. The older boys are with us, but the two younger ones are with her at your brother-in-law's. Nuria is asking for a divorce." His mother looked at him again.

"Son, Nuria is a descent believing woman, and the best wife one can get. How can you do that to yourself?" Ali did not speak, and he did not tell his mother about the fate that awaited him in Isiolo. If his nephew at the county council helped him, he would get at least five years of jail term.

"Son, is it true?"

"What?"

"I've heard that you lost your plot and squandered the government's tax money. Oh, my son, how can you trade your whole life for a Mirra? What will you leave for your children? Is there a curse put on you?" Tears rolled down her cheeks. She wiped them off and sneezed. "We're getting old; who will take care of your children?"

"Mom, I'll be fine. How many cows do I still own?"

She looked up, engulfed with emotions. "You sold all of them. None left."

A week later, as expected, Ali received a sentence of five years in jail.

The Predator

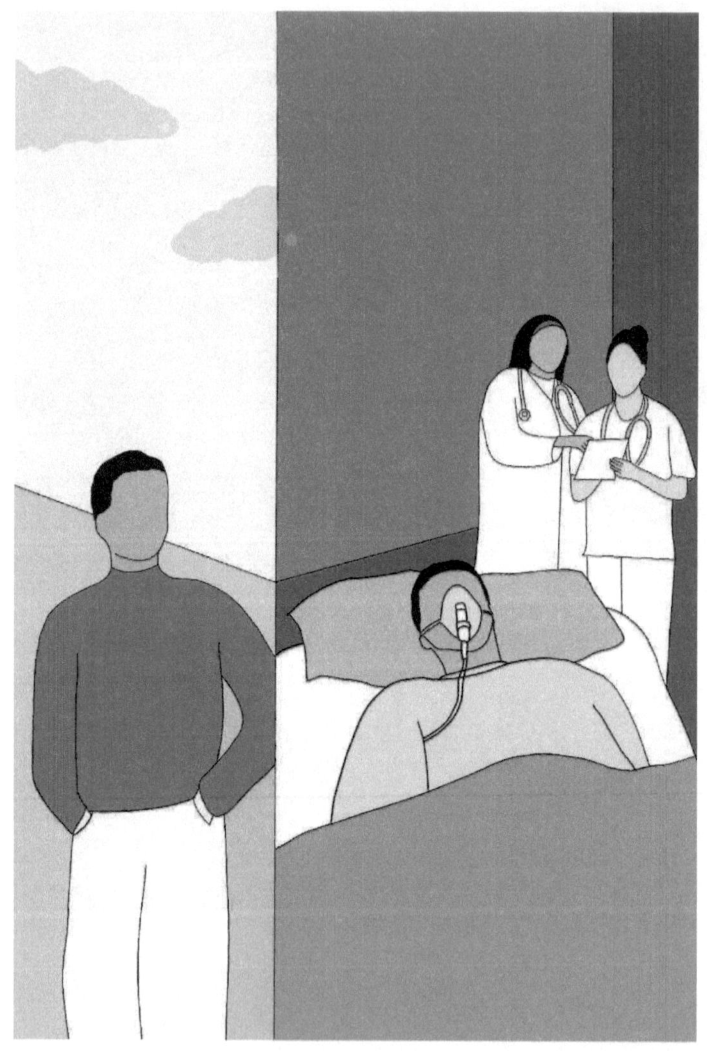

I sa Elemo stopped at chief Habane's retail shop by the bus stop to buy cigarettes. He greeted some customers, as tradition required. The moment he entered the shop, people turned their heads to look at him. Isa looked around the shop at the usual items spread on the shelves.

"You're the best-dressed man I've ever seen or

is there a special occasion today?" a young boy commented.

Isa smiled and gave the boy a ten-shilling note. "Go and buy candy," he nodded with satisfaction, extolling the sort of accolade he craved.

"Nothing special, boy. I have always dressed nicely. Is this the first time you saw me or what? I'm on the way to meet with some friends." Isa abruptly stopped when he saw a lady appear, behind the counter. He looked at her for a moment.

"Oh, you must be the new one in town. Are you?" He asked, looking at her.

Some of the other customers ordered their items, and Isa stepped aside to let them. The young lady walked elegantly in a coquettish manner to the shelf, picked up the items, and handed them. She picked up the brightly colored shawl that dropped on the floor and waited for the next customer to order. Isa kept gazing at her. It must have been a while before he realized the people behind him became impatient. He then moved aside to give them more space again and again.

"It is your turn now. If you still want to go, I guess." She ushered him with the same immaculate gesture that captivated him. Isa gave her a hundred-shilling note for the cigarettes.

"I don't have enough change for that amount." Madina stretched her hand to receive it but hesitated. With the money still in his hand, Isa looked around the shop. Nobody else was behind him in a line.

"Oh, you can keep the change." He murmured. His voice was barely audible.

Not sure what he said, Madina held on to the money and repeated. "You can check the next shop."

"I said, keep it." He nodded.

"What! Keep for what?"

"I mean," he mumbled. "Keep the change."

Madina understood his intentions and placed the money in the envelope, before putting it under the counter. She glanced at him. "How often do you do that to impress a lady?"

Isa shot back with a surprise. "No, I don't do anything to impress anybody, madam. Let me introduce myself. My name is Isa." He held his hand to her across the counter.

"Do you expect me to shake your hand?" With a puzzled look on her face, Madina wondered." I can't shake hands with a person who is not related to me. I guess you know the religious requirements."

Isa held a frozen expression on his face; he'd pretended that he didn't know. Madina wore a hijab, the head cover worn by Muslim ladies, and as a Muslim, he should know about this. She greeted him with a nod of the head. "Nice to meet you. My name is Madina."

"I see. I have heard a lot about you since you arrived in Chari, and now I've witnessed the truth of what people said. I hear people come all the way to look at your beauty. I'm sure you must have heard about me too."

Madina laughed. "Really, why do you think so?"

"As you've seen, this is a small town, and people normally talk and share information. I'm well established in Chari town and very popular." He said with an air of confidence. Madina knew people shared information in a small town. As a medical student, she often helped at the hospital, and people came to her for advice and shared jokes with her. They'd already started calling her Doctor Madina.

Isa then lighted a cigarette and started smoking.

"I would rather have you not smoke here?" she said, raising her hands. Isa didn't expect that gesture. He quickly put off the cigarette.

"You're telling me not to smoke and yet willing to sell me the product? What a paradox."

"I'm not the owner of the products, but there are customers who don't smoke, and we don't need to expose them." Another customer came into the shop and ordered some items. Then an older man with rugged clothing came close to the counter and asked for help. Madina took the money Isa tipped her and handed it to the beggar. Theman opened his eyes wide and exclaimed with gratification.

Isa glanced at Madina, in distaste for what she did, as he left the shop.

He almost knocked into another lady at the door because he was still looking at Madina.

When he arrived at his friend's house, Isa stood for a while. "Mude!" he beckoned to his friend, "I've never seen such a beautiful face in my whole life. What I saw today with my own eyes, the image is still reverberating in my head. I am bewitched!"

"What do you mean?" replied Mude, in a low tone. "You must stop this greed of yours. You're married and have a wonderful young wife, and yet you never change your bad habit. People no longer entertain this kind of behavior that you want to indulge in. Here they observe the faith and follow, and they scoff at the old tradition. The world has changed, my friend. You have to respect your married life. What's wrong with you? Adultery is a sin. You know it." He checked whether anybody was listening. "Besides, some people have not forgiven you. You have caused misery, broken hearts, and disappointments. What makes you think this girl will fall for your whims?"

"I'll try. I instantly fell in love with her and will propose to her." He coughed. "Why do you consider every encounter with a lady a sin *zina.?*"

"You know very well that a lustful look is considered adultery of the eyes. That's why we are encouraged tolower our gazes. You saw her today and already started your fantasy! You want to pop everywhere, like a fly. Every newcomer in the town is the object of your fantasy. Come on Isa, grow up to be a man. You have to stop once and for all." He glanced at him. "By the way, did you check with your doctor about that persistent cough? It's taken you a long time, and you've also lost weight."

"I'm fine. It is just from the smoke. I'll try to minimize it."

Isa liked to shine in the company of his friends. He knew secretly the personal struggle he faced with insecurity and fought hard against the monster within. The inadequacy Isa experienced worsened when his habits caught up with him. He was busy seducing other women and girls until the whole scandal brewed up in his backyard. *How could he ever forgive her.?* The thoughts came back to haunt him every time he fell back into his bad habit. In the end, Isa found relief and didn't even want to admit. Mude suggested that he seek medical help and thought it was compulsive sexual behavior, or what they called hypersexuality, a disease that he was suffering from.

Isa had twin boys. He still remembered the look on his mother's face when his wife gave birth. His mother was angry enough to tell him that the kids did not resemble either his family line or his wife's family. It was obvious. The twins were easy to identify because of their flat nose and thick lips, which was a total contrast to his straight nose, curly hair, and thin lips. He'd never accepted them and knew they were not his children. The twins were born soon after he married. He married his wife without fulfilling the idda, after she got divorced from her previous husband. Isa did not wait for three complete menstrual cycles, as was required before he could marry. As impatient as he was, he broke the rule and married his wife. It was clear from the beginning that she was pregnant when he married her. People quickly forgot the incident until the twins were born, and then rumors started circulating. So Isa decided to punish his wife.

He swore that he'd never come close to her.

The neighbors whispered amongst themselves, they too had observed that Isa's kids looked different, but everyone tightened their lips. They were fed up with his obnoxious lifestyle but disapproved of what they heard, if it was true. Most people didn't know the details and were eager to accept the rumor and move on. Isa heard all that people said about him. The people didn't accuse him directly but would use proverbs to make references about him as they made their points or gave warnings. An elder across from his house used the following local saying to reference Isa's situation. "Jarjaraan hoori hin horu" A hasty person doesn't breed wealth (cows). The proverb implies that a person who doesn't plan carefully, acts recklessly. Such a person will do anything to impress. It could also refer to the offspring.

Later as they sat, Mude and his friends discussed their jobs, Isa's mind kept wandering. He pictured Madina in his head. In the past, when he sat with his friends to talk, some of them would discuss politics and women, and Isa would become energized with excitement. He'd narrate and narrate his exploits and boast of all the adventures he had encountered. He had a strange way of showing off how successful he was in his endeavors and how everybody adored him. Some of his critics did not believe all that he said and brushed him off. Isa also attracted scandals.

"You know the new dame in town. She's so critical about what some of us are doing. I understand that she refused to shake hands with men," said Duba.

"What else do you know about her?"

Isa glanced at Mude.

"They say she's religious."

"What do you mean?" asked Isa.

"I don't know Isa," shrugged Duba, "But I heard that she condemns all forms of immorality, adultery, and blames women for stooping so low."

"Mude, just give me a week. She is no different," commented Isa, as he lit a cigarette.

Over the years, he'd acquired a reputation for earning the title of the best-dressed man and was notorious for womanizing almost every woman he saw. He claimed that they could not resist him and even attributed his success to a charm that he possessed; wherever he met with his friends, he would talk and extoll his adventures and future jobs. He did all the tricks he could, to convince some girls who were just out of school, promising them a career in government ministries. As it turned out, he never delivered the promised jobs. In some quarters, wherever you mentioned his name, some people would turn their heads away in disgust. Isa did the most despicable things to expose the sins he committed and allowed everybody to know without shame. He'd boast to his friends and openly showed them the lists of names and records of his activities that he kept.

Isa returned to the chief's shop later in the day. Madina saw him as he entered but did not raise her head to look at him. She kept reading a magazine.

"You forgot this," She gave him a key holder.

"Oh, that's where I left." He picked up the key holder he'd deliberately left behind in the first place. Isa stayed in the shop until the sunset. He talked with Madina about his job with the Ministry of Natural resources. Madina also shared with him her life activities at her second-year medical school. She told him that she would like to come to Chari hospital and practice her medicine after college. And Isa kept telling her about the adventures and activities that he had accomplished in the area.

"Nice to meet you again. I will close the shop now."

"Go ahead and close. I enjoyed talking with you." He hesitated. "You know, I am wondering. This is a small town where everybody knows each other. I would like to come back later tonight after sunset. You see, from the time I saw you, my mind was not the same. I am deeply in love with you, and I'm seriously considering a proposal." He paused.

Madina turned to face him and laughed.

"You think I'm a high school girl? You know that I'm engaged. Don't you?" she asked.

"Ya, what?" he mumbled, taken aback by the unexpected question, "Don't pretend that you're stranger to cultural habits."

"Of course, I'm not new to the area, but I choose not to normalize the wrong and sins. I wonder why you're not ashamed of your actions. You have a wife and two children. How can you face them?" Madina looked at him in the eyes. "I consider your request an insult." She paused. "You have come to the wrong person. I don't appreciate this kind of behavior. This concludes my discussions with you. Get out!" She ordered him.

Isa resisted. "No woman has ever or will ever speak to me like that. You've humiliated me and will pay for this." He added.

"I say get out now, before I call my uncle." She stood firm. "You don't want to cause a scene, I guess." She walked to the door, but Isa came from behind her. He grabbed her and turned her around to face him. He held her face with both of his hands.

"What are you trying to do?" She pushed him away as he was tightening his grip.

"What do you expect?”

He suddenly pulled her head towards his mouth.

Madina pulled away with all the forces she could garner. She freed her head and stood at a distance from him. "If you come closer to me, I will scream and use any means available to me. You filthy brute, try that again, and you'll see!" She picked up a log from nearby the door, ready to strike if approached.

Isa banged the door behind him and left.

The next day Isa invited his friends to a local restaurant. As usual, their discussions centered on local politics and social lives. "Wait, I have to tell you this." He sipped a cold soda to interrupt the hiccup. "It did not take me a week, as I thought. The new bird in town is now mine." His three friends scooted forward to hear more.

"How did you manage it?" asked Mude.

He'd heard from some other people that Madina was stringent and did not entertain nonsense.She was the most decent girl anybody could imagine. However, all of them were curious to find out about this new development.

Isa appeared elusive in his answers. He avoided direct answers and talked on general issues. He told them in detail how he had a wonderful time with her in the shop and how he'd remained in the shop after everybody had gone. He told them that he later came back, and she opened the shop in the evening for him. He used the backdoor to enter the shop again. He said she welcomed his proposal with eagerness and high interest. Those who knew Isa would take half of what he said and filter them. His three friends looked at each other, and none dare to confront him. He paid for their lunches and bundles of Mirra, which they started chewing.

The evening dragged on, as they listened to Isa's self-glorification. His friends didn't want to offend him. He paid for all their expenses and the extravagance they had indulged in. Among his friends, only Mohammed ever questioned him.

"She agreed so easily?" inquired Mohammed.

"Yes, so easy. Just like that." He clicked his tongue to indicate the swiftness with which he'd accomplished his work. "She initiated it. I was rather surprised."

"Well, Isa, we've heard a lot about your exploits, politics, women, and social issues. How many times have we ever talked about solving any of those problems we talked about?" continued Mohammed, nodding his head, "Society condones all the unusual things that we do, yet we all know that it's wrong to commit adultery. Suppose it was your wife? I'm sure you wouldn't like it. I suggest we cease from such discussions and rumors again. Besides, you're talking about significant abominable sins. Things you should not even speak in public. It's a disgrace, and I don't know why we have to listen to this filthy talk. Madina is an honorable lady, and I am ready to defend her reputation. I cannot just watch and allow you to degrade our women. I will not be part of it."

Mohammed stopped and they all sat quietly. Nobody talked for what seemed to be a long time.

"What's wrong with you, man? If you don't want to be my friend, you're free to go. I will not regard you as a friend anymore." Isa commented.

The group dispersed shortly afterward, but Mude and Isa remained behind. "What's wrong with Mohammed?"

Mude did not respond. He knew Isa would not like to hear the truth, so Mude prepared to leave.

The next day, the rumor of Isa's encounter with Madina spread through the little town. By the time Madina figured out what happened, her fiancé, who was in Nairobi at a distance of over 600 kilometers away, had also known about the whole story of Isa's flirtation with his fiancées. Mohammed had called him as soon as he heard what Isa said and told him everything that he heard and made it clear that it was a lie.

Madina posted a letter to her fiancé before the incident with Isa happened and was contemplating sending him another letter to explain what transpired. She knew how the rumor mongers twisted words and created tales of deceptions.

Madina came from another town, and Chari was her fiancé's town, as well as her uncle's, who was the local chief. Madina likes to help her uncle in the shop whenever she visited. He paid part of her college tuition, and she wanted to help him during the vacation.

Later, Madina met with her friend Hawo. "I can't believe he said that about you. The whole town's talking about it."

"I am not worried. I know myself, just ignore him."

"Madina, you cannot ignore this," exclaimed her friend, casting a worried gaze, "It's about your reputation. You're chaste, and this incident is tantamount to defiling your virtues and honor."

"My dear friend, by fanning this, we're giving him the publicity he craves for. But Isa has never met his match, and a typical narcissist individual like him with an inflated sense of his importance would thrive on this kind of atmosphere. He's sick and needs excessive attention and admiration. I won't give him that attention."

Hawo pulled her down. "Clear your mind. What about Huqa? He would probably hear Isa's version of the story and doubt you." Madina smiled.

"I'll send him a letter to explain everything. I had to contradict myself about the previous message. I highly praised the generosity of the people in this town, and even innocently mentioned that Isa was his competitor." Hawo covered her mouth in shock.

"No way, Madina. This will make him suspicious. I have an idea. We can use Mohammed, Huqa, trusts him."

"Hawo, it isn't necessary. I'm confident, and Huqa will not fall for this cheap vibe."

Madina and her fiancé Huqa were very open to each other. They shared jokes and any little information that one of them thought interesting. Before they were even engaged, they promised each other to set a good example to others by staying loyal and faithful to each other. Not a single thought had ever crossed her mind that she would break the promise. Besides, as a firm believer in the Islamic faith, she had no room in her heart for anything that would make her go against the marriage matrimony she vowed to keep.

She sat down in the corner of the shop and composed another letter to her fiancé. She explained to him the rumors she heard and how out of her ignorance and naïveté, she became a victim of a devious predator. "You probably heard the shocking news, but with God as my witness. I've nothing to dishonor our vow." She wrote with emotion; her tears soaked the paper as it trickled down. Then Madina sealed the envelope and took a deep breath. She wondered about what Hawo said about her reputation.

Madina then returned to the shop counter to help. A little girl handed her a package with a note. Madina stretched her hand to receive the package, but then she withdrew it and instead asked the girl who sent the package. Having been cautioned and familiar with the secret courting system rampant in the area, the girl did not want to disclose who gave her the parcel. She left it on the counter.

Madina opened the note and dropped it. She bust into tears.

She sobbed. "Why does Isa want to destroy me? Why?" At that time, the chief, her uncle, entered the shop and observed the commotion. Madina had no time to reposition herself.

"Dad," she wiped tears with her sari and looked up. The chief was her father's brother, and as the tradition requires, she called him father. The chief thought something drastic happened to her and waited for her to regain composure. "This man is dishonoring me. He's spread lies and is tainting my reputation. He sends me gifts, which I refused." She pointed to the package the little girl left behind.

The chief called the little girl, who confirmed that Isa sent her to deliver the package: sari, beads, bungles, and perfume.

The chief knew Isa very well, and the past scandals associated with him were still fresh in his mind. He gave Madina a fatherly pat. " Let me handle this." He told her in low tones to stay in the house. He then turned to the girl.

"Tell him to come to the shop." He picked up the gifts and kept it in a corner.

Shortly after, the chief sent the package with one of his sons. "Take it to where it belongs," he instructed.

Isa came home late that evening and found his wife crying. She cursed him as soon as she saw him; he knew it was one of the news about him that she was concerned with. Halima had already told him that she would leave him if he ever got involved with another woman again. She knew he had been fishing around as she called his adultery habits, but it did not occur to her that she had enough excuses to leave him. He denied all the charges, although his behaviors indicated that he had committed some mischievous acts. She'd even suggested to him to get a second or third wife if he needed it. He looked around; there were some boxes on the floor. The children were already with her mother in Nakuru town. Since he knew the children were not his, Halima excluded him from all the decisions concerning them. She took the children to her mother whenever the school was closed.

"What! Going on a trip?"

He asked, ignoring her curses.

"Yes, a long trip. I will not live with you anymore. I'm transferring my teaching job to Nakuru and will leave this town tonight."

She threw a package to him. He recognized the parcel and kept quiet.

"How far can you go?" she asked, with disgust, "Madina is one of the most respectable ladies, I've ever known. You don't have a marriage, but why destroy somebody else's? Our life together never existed. But I just wanted you to know one thing, unlike you, I've always been faithful."

Isa did not speak. He recognized the package he'd sent to Madina. He turned it over and at one corner was a hand-scribbled note that said, "Go to hell, where you belong!"

***

The next day Mude came to Isa's house. It was 10.00 am, and Isa was alone in the house. "Hey, man! You look terrible. What happened?" Mude asked.

Isa coughed. "She's gone."

Mude looked around the house; there was nothing much to see. "I don't know how to tell you about this, but the whole town is sickened by what you did. I just wished that you kept it to yourself. The chief has organized the tribal elders to seek compensation for the damages you caused. He's using the traditional laws against you."

"What? Who would listen to his archaic customary laws? For how long will he cling to dying tradition?" mocked Isa, unabashed.

Chief Habane had managed to keep the society together. Wherever necessary, he had utilized the elders to administer their traditional laws as needed. Except for serious crimes, he tried to practice the tribal rules in the rural areas. The community lived in harmony, and in most cases, all the crimes were punishable by thrashing or fining. After consulting with some of the elders, the chief conclude that Isa deserved a punishment. According to the traditional punishment scale, dishonoring an unmarried girl is a serious crime, with a fine even up to 30 cattle. The chief had vowed to use the customary laws to claim 30 animals from Isa. Chief Habane had enforced the rules in the past. Isa and Mude thought the chief inflated the number of cows and wondered how he came up with fine of thirty cows.

They believed that he had no right to the claim, however, the onus of facing the crowd remained with Isa. He had no other choice. The elders would squeeze Isa's father, who still adhered to the traditional values, and if confronted, Isa's old man would never go against the wishes of the tribe.

Mude cleared his voice. "You'll have to tell the truth about what happened and face the consequences." As he prepared to leave, Isa coughed again. Mude looked at him closely. "Is that real blood that you spit? How long have you had this?"

Isa's silence prompted him to wait. "I have a fever, and I need to see a doctor today." He'd finally given in.

Isa was still very much indoors for the next couple of days. He went to the clinic, where the doctor took some blood samples and sent it to the district hospital. In the meantime, Isa stayed with Mude. The people in the town had divided opinions about the incident Isa caused. The chief had already filed the case against him, and the elders met and decided on the fine because Isa refused to attend and defend himself.

The day Isa's blood result came back from the district hospital, Madina was at the clinic, helping nurses as she did in the past. She'd handled some patients' file and freely conducted her duties as if she was a doctor. The doctor had called Isa to review with him the results. Isa entered the office; but didn't expect Madina to be there. She brought his file to the doctor and closed the door behind her.

Isa froze. "Why does she have my file? I have the right to privacy." He stood up to leave.

"Sit down," the doctor ordered with a stern voice, and Isa obeyed.

"I have the results of your tests," he waited for Isa to settle. Madina sensed how uncomfortable he felt and decided to leave the room, but the doctor told her to stay. "I want you to write down for me the names of all the women you had contact with, in the past."

Isa pulled back. "Are you out of your mind? I came to get the results of my medical test. What has this got to do with my private life? I have the right to remain silent," he fumed, avoiding Madina's eyes.

The doctor calmed him down. "Isa, listen carefully, and this is especially important. This information will remain here, and we will not disclose the nature of your disease. Please, just do as I say. I would like to know the names of all the women you've had encounters with." He pleaded with him. "We have to test them."

"Why?" asked Isa, as he broke down in tears, "Don't tell me that I have that dreadful disease? Just tell me it's not that one." The doctor held him back to a seat.

"The preliminary tests indicate that you have tested positive. We will conduct some more tests to confirm it fully. Do you understand why I need the names of the women you've had contact with?" The doctor insisted.

The doctor decided to have him watched twenty-four hours a day until he settled. He was on a watch list for a suicide attempt.

Unaware of the turmoil in Isa's life, the rest of the world continued with their daily lives. Isa provided a long list of names, and for the next several days, the hospital representatives contacted all those women whose names he provided. The doctor worked closely with Madina. She took the role of counselor and increased her involvement in the educational process. The lack of knowledge about some of the diseases and the general ignorance contributed by the sexual promiscuity of the traditional ways of life had made it difficult. Madina volunteered to conduct educational programs about Aids and other sexually transmitted diseases.

But in a small town like Chari, secrets were hard to hide, and the rumor about Isa's strange disease got leaked out. Some people had accepted his version of the story. He told some of his close friends that he was under a spell of love magic cast upon him and tested positive for Tuberculosis (TB).

Madina approached the bed where Isa slept. He raised his head.

Isa looked so much different from the person she saw a few days ago. He was not even looking her in the eyes. With his eyes downcast, Isa cupped his chin with his right hand and supported himself on his elbow.

Madina came closer to his bed; they were other patients on the opposite side of the beds arranged in rows of twos. She stood at a distance, wondering whether to come closer to him or not. She heard about some HIV positive patients who committed evil acts by maliciously infecting other people. She heard of a man who took a loan and went on a spending spree, giving it to women, to seek unwanted favors. They said he approached prominent women and seduced them. That it was evil and heinous crimes that no human being could ever imagine doing, but some people could commit such crimes. After a little hesitation, she offered him a nod of greeting. Isa lowered his gaze in humiliation. She talked with him and reassured him that everything would be okay. The nurse joined them; it was time for his medication. Isa was kept under vigil for the next two weeks.

"Isa, everything is in the hands of God. I will pray for your quick recovery. Please accept what you cannot change for now and be easy on yourself." Madina said.

The following week Isa received a note Mude brought to him at the hospital, by his wife. She came to visit him after she'd heard what happened. Mude told him in the letter that the chief had dropped the charges against him. He also narrated to him that some people had known about the nature of his illness. Isa threw the letter under the bed. "He is just in town, and yet he has to write me a letter instead of visiting me?" Isa murmured. None of the people he considered friends had visited him so far. He was shocked, and as each day went by, he realized that he had no real friends anymore.

He concluded that life was not worth living.

"How are you doing?" his wife asked again. She had seen how he looked, and the doctor had already talked with her. "I tested negative," she announced. He sat still with vacant eyes focusing on the ceiling of the room. "Don't hurt yourself," she advised. "I'm sorry about this. I have to go now." Halima approached the nurse and talked with her in low tones.

The nurse looked towards Isa and shook her head.

Later that evening, Isa pushed the button to call a nurse and Madina approached him.

"I know you won't forgive me. But I just wanted to say that I'm sorry about what I did to you."

Madina stood silent for a while and spoke. "Okay, I will make du'a for you. May Allah grant you recovery. Trust in Him and seek forgiveness. Here," She gave him a copy of the Quran to read. "I'll be leaving town soon. Good luck, and don't give up. It's possible to recover from this disease." She advised.

SWEET & SOUR

iro noticed Hassan, his nephew, as he was about to leave for his dinner. Hassan opened the door to his room quickly and shut it when he saw him. Giro shook his head and ignored him.
"He's probably drugged as usual. What a low life to lead."

"Are you talking to me?" His wife, Jamila, came behind him to lock the door.

Giro pointed with his mouth, "Is he still around?"

"Who?"

He directed his gaze towards the room where his nephew lived.

"He'll be gone, all right, and won't be a burden to you anymore. Don't worry."

"Remember, I gave him all the chances. If he acts stupid again, I will not rescue him. He must complete his jail term. That might be better for him than here." Giro added, and turned around. "Tell me. How many times did he get caught? Five? Why can't he learn from his dumb mistakes? Using drugs is for losers."

Giro prepared to leave, and Jamila looked after him. She turned towards the room where Hassan lived and hesitated, not wanting to entertain further dawdling. Finally, Jamila knocked on the door twice and twisted the doorknob. She waited. "Who is it?" Hassan asked.

"It's me. Open!"

"Oh" Hassan opened the door and stood in the doorway: he gestured at the room, "I'm packing."

"You're going somewhere?"

"What do you think?" he scoffed, leaning against the doorway, "I'm not wanted here. So, what am I supposed to do?"

Jamila always had a soft spot for him, Hassan and her younger brother were close friends, and they went to the same boarding school, which was why she considered him like her brother.

"Where I go is nobody's business."

He stepped back into the room and continued packing. Jamila heard him said a similar thing before. "I hope this time you're right, but you can stay. You can get your job back, you know. Our only concern is your habits. If you control your bad habits, you can stay if you want." Hassan looked up when she mentioned the word habit. He laughed mockingly; his uncle told him the same thing when he fired him from the manager's position at his restaurant.

"I've had enough. Don't worry about my addiction. The days for your corrupt husband are nearing."

"Listen," said Jamila, shocked to hear him talk about his uncle in that manner. "Is this the way you thank us? Whatever my husband does is none of your business. He provides a decent living for his family. He gave you a job, you blew it up and saved you from jail time too. What else can he do for you?"

"I'm in a hurry now." He stopped packing and waited. "You take care. He loves those smuggled goods more than he loves you. Where do you think your husband gets all the wealth he has? He stole from the government. He used people to steal for him. All those goods he smuggled into the country and the wildlife trophies. What do you think? All those are legal?"

"Stop it!" She raised her hand.

"There is no difference between what I do and what he does. He did not serve a jail term yet, probably that's the only difference. But trust me, there's a lot that you don't know about your husband."

"I say cut it loose, young man! He never forged papers to steal from the bank. He never used the drug and got caught."

"Stop right there," replied Hassan, shaking his head at her, "People who eat from the same plate think alike. I can see where you're heading. Yes, they caught me. Are you saying that it would have been okay if I was not caught? I know how both of you think. You're more concerned about your image and reputations."

He paused, about to continue rambling, but Jamila had already closed the door and walked away.

***

At the Sun Restaurant, hotel, and nightclub, the nightlife had begun.

Giro slipped the brown envelope under the table. "Catch this," he lowered his voice. "As we agreed; everything is as planned." He then grabbed his soda and sipped it. "Your boys did a wonderful job. They got their share all right."

John Karani, the District Commissioner (DC), winked with satisfaction as he took the envelope. He placed the package between his muscular thighs and secured it with his knees. He didn't need to count the amount. Giro would do as he promised. They sat for a while and enjoyed the evening with all kinds of entertainment. John poured himself a glass of his favorite drink; tilting it, he poured the frothy liquid along the wall of the glittering glass to minimize the foam. He filled it slowly and quickly sipped before it overflowed. Tunde, the attendant, approached the table.

"Let her do it," Giro advised.

And with some extra glasses in hand, Tunde took over from John. She then wiped the foam off the glass and the table.

"You see, that's her job," Giro commented, keeping his gaze on the attendant.

Tunde picked up the empty bottles, wiped the table, and waited for further instructions. Giro dismissed her and quickly left the room, leaving the door ajar. The restaurant and the boarding section of the building were all connected. A few of the rooms, adjacent to the restaurant across the hall, were all rented to the individual customers. One would cross an open area from the hallway where customers sat and waited for their turns to get served.

A little distance, at a corner of the free space, Tunde moved Juda Tambo, the District Commissioner's bodyguard, to a different location. She set his table to face the door of the room where Giro and DC sat. Juda did not wear a uniform, but Giro and some customers knew the DC would not go out in the night without a bodyguard, especially when he expected some documents from Giro. Juda sipped soda and munched ugali with beef stew. He wore an overall coat that concealed his revolver.

As Tunde refilled his drink, he leaned over and whispered to her; she went to the shelf at the counter and brought him a packet of Marlboro. He lit the cigarette and continued with his evening feast. Tunde scribbled the price on the paper. She would later add the bills together with the DC's and put them into a separate envelope for Giro to take care of.

She looked around for the hotel manager, who was busy with customers. Tunde stooped, pretending to pick up a paper and dropped a key. Juda covered it with his foot, incognizant of what he concealed under his foot, the other customers around him, called Tunde for more services.

"Room 16. It's under the bed. Use the back door with the other key. The watchman is not there. Now is the time," she whispered. Tunde picked up the bottles and left Juda's table to attend to other customers.

Giro and John conversed, out of the hearing range. But Tunde checked on them often, picking up empty bottles and bringing fresh ones to their table. She would clean the table, wait to receive orders, and leave the room.

Friday evening was usually a busy night; the patrons were already gathered before the social hours began.

While Giro left for the bathroom, John Karani stretched himself up. The parcel still held by his knees fell to the floor; he'd almost forgotten about it. He picked up the brown, tightly sealed envelope. He then took a penknife and peeped through the tiny opening and looked at the content in bewilderment. He dipped his hand into the depth of the envelope and scooped out the contents. He withdrew bundles of papers. He looked at one wrapped package, then another and another until all the tightly tied bundles were out of the envelope. He stood gazing at the papers. John hadn't noticed when Giro return.

"What's this supposed to mean?" growled John, shaking the bundles at Giro, "Is it April fool's day or what?"

"What!" Giro exclaimed, bustling closer, "Oh, God! It can't be true." He picked up the blank papers tied into a bundle. "These are empty papers!" He held the papers up and turned them over and over.

John did not speak. He tapped the table with his knuckles and wiped off some drops of sweat.

"Well, this doesn't look good. How many people are you dealing with?"

Giro gazed in shock. "No, No, it's not what you think. I work alone and only with you. I'll sort out this mess. It must be an inside theft. I'll take care of it." He paused, taking the envelope from John, "You'll get your parcel tomorrow as promised. And I'll make sure that this kind of error never happen again." Giro left quickly. He called the manager aside and whispered to him.

Tunde moved about in the open spaces and continuously checked on the boss, making sure that everything he needed was in place. She noticed Giro pacing back and forth; when he saw her, he turned and charged towards her.

"Tunde! Wait for me in my office. But check on John first and make sure he has everything he needs." Giro used one room at the hotel as an office.

Tunde knocked on the door and entered. John Karani turned around to face her. "Hi, Tunde."

He grabbed her by the hip and made her sit on his lap; then he started rocking back and forth to the tune of Lingala music in the background. Tunde pushed him aside as he prepared to fondle her under her apron. "I have to go. No time for dance or mischief."

"Where is your boss?" he asked, looking at her, "Tell me. Do you fool around with him too?"

She shifted, but he turned her around. "That was a dumb question. I should've known. Anyways, I want to know if I could trust you."

"With what?" she asked.

"You know I could be handy for you. I want you to do some favors for me. Just between you and me, and I'll take good care of you," he whispered, with a smile.

Tunde understood that kind of smile. She'd been used and misused by many, but she needed all the extra money she could get to educate her sister. John had sought favors from her, and he often got what he wanted. At first, Tunde thought she would be the usual mistress, unofficial wife, and she knew many women who had played that role, but John's favor went beyond the ordinary. It never occurred to her that John could stoop so low. On several occasions, he paid her to do favors for his friends as well. She was a conduit through which John acquired his other personal favors. A degrading moment she loathed, but she fulfilled all his requests because of the promise he made to her. As one of the highest-ranking government officials in the district, DC had all the powers. At least she was glad he got her a plot of residential land. He also promised to connect her sister to a job opportunity with a company controlled by his friends.

"How close are you with Giro?"

"What do you want to know?"

"I need to know his business partners; you know the business I have in mind."

Tunde smiled. She took out a paper from her pocket and wrote down a few names, handing it to him. "Do you recognize these names?" John grabbed the paper from her, but before he opened it, he heard footsteps approaching. He squeezed the note between his palm and waited.

Giro entered and Tunde left the room quietly.

***

Giro called all 17 of his employees. He met with them individually. The manager, Mr. Asante, had already told them about the impending meeting without disclosing the urgent meeting's purpose at the late hours of the night.

All of them left the meeting with their heads down. They felt a tragedy had befallen them, as an evil person now lived among them. Giro looked all of them over; some of them had tears in their eyes. They were frightened and shocked that they would no longer trust their colleagues anymore.

"Boss, I don't know what to say; you're the only one who has the keys. You always carried one, and I guess you left it at home." The manager reminded Giro politely.

"I know that," he replied, looking at him with a leer. "You're not suggesting that I stole my own money."

"No, sir."

"The room is not locked when I'm around! Any of the employees can slip in and do whatever they wanted to do. I may have to fire all of you." Giro pulled the handle of the door to close it. Mr. Asante was barely making it out before the door banged on him. The vibration of the banging door rattled the papers on the table. Asante opened his mouth, but words failed to come out.

"So-oory sir...I will do a thorough investigation." He mumbled.

That night Giro tossed on the bed. His wife had noticed his erratic behavior, but he did not talk when he arrived home. The first thing he asked for was the extra key to his office, and quickly checked in the drawer where he placed it. The key was in place. After a long silence, he sighed.

"I'm sure Hassan doesn't have access to my key?"

He held the key up to show her.

"No, why?"

She waited to hear what he would say.

"A parcel is missing from my office."

"I don't think he could do something like that. He's an addict but not a thief," she snapped.

Giro kept quiet.

"Are you all right?" she asked.

"Yes, Yes! I'm all right."

"What else? She insisted.

Jamila waited; she knew something was not right and had a feeling that it had to do with the business. Giro did not involve her in any decisions concerning his business dealings, but Jamila had lived with him for ten years and knew everything he did. She could read his moods. It looked as if something terrible had happened, and she almost sensed that it had to do with the secret activities that he'd gotten involved in.

Over the years, Jamila had seen tons of items stored at her home. Some of them included banned wildlife trophies (leopard skin, ivory, & rhino horns. And as the years passed, his business expanded, and he built rental houses, hotels, restaurants, and nightclubs. For those who don't know him well, Giro's business was legitimate because he actively participated in running his place in the town. Still, Jamila was mostly worried about his other illicit source of income. She noticed the large sums of money he kept at home. But Giro brushed her off when she expressed concern about the danger it could pose to their lives if burglars broke into the house. He only assured her that nothing would happen. Giro must have seen her point because after she talked about the security, he employed an extra watchman to guard his home. Jamila knew what was going around. She had her eyes and ears wide open. Workers have confided in her, and some employees, hoping to gain her favors, volunteered some information with her. It was mostly about money that Jamila wanted to know.

As a stay home mother of five and with several maids and help around the house, she had plenty of time for gossip. Jamila would be the first to wear the latest fashion imported from Dubai. She adored her fingers with precious ornaments. Diamonds were her favorite, and she showed off the sparkling stones as she gracefully paraded them on her earlobes.

Giro had no problem meeting her material needs, but his friction with her was about her strong protective support for Hassan, his nephew, who was a drug addict. Giro didn't want to sustain him, although he had kept him out of prison with his friends' help at the police station several times. At one time, he even made him a manager of one of his hotels. But Hassan had become a nuisance to the extent that Giro wanted him out of his house.

Several days and weeks following the disappearance of Giro's two hundred and fifty thousand shillings, life at the hotel and restaurant continued as usual. There were many new faces, and previous employees, including the manager, got fired. Tunde survived the ax and retained her job.

There was no trace of the money and no lead. Giro could not bring the police into the matter for investigation. He would rather forget the money ever existed than bear the exposure of illegal funds. He knew he would gain more. However, Giro secretly continued to investigate who got away with the money. *If I ever catch the culprit, I'll boil him alive.* He thought.

Tunde dusted off the table in the hotel room. She lifted the curtain just enough to see through the window; underneath the trees, she noticed some movements. It was still dark, and she couldn't figure out who the people were and what they were doing. The shadowy figures waited behind the trees. Then she saw Giro joined them. At that moment, she heard footsteps approaching the door. She then quickly prepared the bed and left the room. Tunde continued with her work. It was not a busy night, and only her frequent customers had arrived. She occupied her usual position. Giro came with three visitors and went straight to the office. Tunde served John Karani, Giro, and another man she never saw before. He had a room reserved in case any of his visitors stayed overnight.

Juda took his place at the usual table and looked around. Tunde brought his drinks and wiped the table. He asked. "Is he here today?" Juda usually came alone, although occasionally he would drive DC's government Land Rover and park it away in the corner near the edge of bushes because it was against the rules to use government vehicles for personal use. His boss would often use his private car, and Juda's duty was to keep an eye on him.

"He is here, right?" Juda whispered as he looked at the newspaper, pretending to read.

"Yes, with another man I've not seen before," Tunde responded without looking at him.

"He is the new secret agent. They have to bring him into the circle as well," he murmured, as he sipped the drinks, " I escorted their cargo yesterday from the forest, past the police barrier, and parked the Landrover. I had to guide the car whole night, and I'll have to escort them out of the district, tomorrow. We'll use the government vehicle and a hospital ambulance. No one would trace anything back to them."

"Are you all right?" asked Tunde, wiping the spotless table.

Juda concentrated on the drink. "Just one time, and that's it." He murmured. "Your boss wants me to do a job for him."

"What kind of a job?" Tunde wiped the table again.

"I'm not sure whether I'd do it anyway." He didn't want her to know the type of work Giro had asked him to do.

"We need to talk," Tunde said.

"I know, I'll be at your place tonight." He picked up the glass and sipped the soda again; his eyes were still guarding the entrance.

"Look!" she whispered, collecting the empty bottles, "That's the man I told you, and he's looking for Hassan. I don't like the way he looks." Juda turned around slowly. He then continued drinking as he had been doing. "Keep an eye on him." He said without looking at her.

Tunde fixed a cocktail, pouring the mixture into a glass. She added drops of soda and ice cubes, and finally placed a straw in the tall glass, before carrying it to Giro's table. John Karani grabbed her by the dress and pulled her closer to where he sat, as she was about to leave. She obeyed the pressure.

"Tunde, come closer." He then mumbled something into her ears. John Karani appeared intoxicated. By any standard, the behavior he depicted was low. Tunde had come across several bizarre incidences of such behavior when men drenched themselves with all kinds of toxic substances. She'd observed some of them pass out and pee in public. The person of DC's rank and reputation should not have behaved the way John did, but Tunde had seen it all. He followed her to the door on his way out to the bathroom.

"Tunde, we need to talk before I go home tonight. Okay!"

"I have an urgent thing to attend to now. I'll stop by." She lied to put him off. John released her hand. Tunde moved on. At the corner of his eyes, Juda looked at his boss with disgust.

***

The customers left one by one, but Tunde was in no hurry; she cleared the last table and took a break.

"Tunde," Giro called her aside. "I understand some people were asking for Hassan. Do you know what they want?

"I don't know, but I guess he might've owed them some money or something. Do you know where he is?" She asked him.

"No, Tunde. To tell you the truth, I am glad he is gone." He said the last word with a bitter tone.

"The money that disappeared."

"What about it?"

"Tunde! Has he anything to do with it?"

"No, it may be just a coincidence. Hassan left before the money disappeared."

"I thought over this for a long time, but he claimed that he was too intoxicated to pull off anything like it. The incident still puzzles me up to this day."

"The person, who asked for him left a number," she wrote a call box number registered in Nyeri and handed him a note. "It was a public booth near the post office."

"Thanks, Tunde. Would you recognize the man if you saw him?"

"Ya," she hesitated.

"What? Are you sure!" He pressed.

"I'm sure, for the last two weeks he's been coming to the restaurant. He has unique features, with a big, deep, dented scar on the right cheek and missing two lower teeth. A unique feature that you won't forget. I saw him today."

"Are you sure? Was he alone?" He took a handkerchief and wiped the sweat from his face. "Close the door and have a seat."

"I think he's booked at our hotel." Tunde watched the unusual behavior of her boss. He moved about and suddenly became agitated; almost frightened. He pulled out a drawer and opened a small bottle and gulped two or three drops.

"If you wanted, I could find out for you." She offered to help.

"Thanks for your help. I just feel exhausted."

"Let me," Tunde massaged his shoulder muscles. She loosened his cloth and continued relaxing his body. She had done that for him in the past, and Giro found her techniques very comforting. With a soft, tender touch and meticulous dexterity, Tunde induced him to sleep. She had a way of making him feel at home. She could give him all the care he desired. She knew what to do, and Giro had come to depend on her for advice as well.

Later that night, Tunde met with Juda at her house. When he arrived, he went straight to the bathroom and washed. He then changed into new clothes that he kept at her house. She noticed some bruises on his hands and marks like nail scratches.

After several minutes, Juda joined her. "It's tomorrow. I found the dealer, a businessman from Mombasa. It turned out to be the same man that I delivered the cargo to the other time. I could meet with him in Nairobi. He used different names. They said he had a passport from all the East African countries and some West African countries as well."

"Do you trust him?" Tunde asked.

"Nobody trusts each other in this business, but we all understand one thing." He glanced at her. "We made sure not to get caught and never disclosed the sources of our products. So, I expect him not to question where I got the products."

"Do you mean you'll escort the cargo tomorrow to Nairobi to the same person?" Juda understood her confusion. He'd delivered the illegal trophies for Giro and John Karani, to a warehouse in Nairobi. His job was to protect the cargo in transit. As a police officer, driving a government vehicle, he was not subjected to inspection. It just happened by accident that the person he delivered the goods to mentioned that he also needed marijuana (Cannabis Sativa).

Tunde pulled out the mattress and retrieved several packages from it. Juda counted ten bundles that weighed about two kilograms each and put it in an empty bag he carried. They would not expect to get less than three Million Shillings with a bargain and the right target. Juda had researched the market for marijuana at the coast, where many tourists visited. He was sure to get more than that estimate, but he would be willing to let it go for a lower price since he got it cheap. "Here," He handed her some money from the previous sale. Tunde had teamed up with Juda, and their secret deal started when Hassan was a manager. She connected Hassan with a marijuana dealer. Tunde held on to her bargain and wanted to be the middle person. She got the deal, but Hassan abandoned the plan for hard drugs and failed on his promise. Then Juda came along and liked the idea; after all, he had the means to dispose of the products.

***

Tunde woke up the next day to a hard knock on her door. A shaken hotel employee came in. "Calm down. Say it slowly," Tunde demanded.

"They slit his throat opened. Oh, what a gruesome savage sight to watch. The police officers are everywhere around the hotel."

"Who is the man?" Tunde asked impatiently.

"A customer! They say he has a scar on the cheek."

"What can I do for you?" Tunde asked again.

"Nothing, your friend said, she saw the man talk with you."

"Look here, Helen, people talk with us all the time around here. It's the nature of our daily work, but I don't recall any specific person."

"Oh, I thought you needed to know," she whimpered.

Tunde closed the door behind her and sat down. A lot of things passed through her mind, which made her shiver.

Later in the day, the police investigators interviewed all the employees at the restaurant and hotel. But just before she met with the police investigator, Giro called her aside.

"Tunde, the police will look for any small thing. They will consider anything you say. So be careful about what you tell them. I don't want any scandal around here. You'll probably be better off if you denied ever seeing him, whoever this person is." He said.

The police interviewed Tunde last. They seemed to know more about this gentleman, but she had little to offer other than what everybody had said. However, for a strange reason, she suspected that they didn't believe her. They asked her why he had her name in her notebook, and they also wanted to know whether her boss knew about this stranger. Tunde had learned a life lesson, and she knew how to keep away from police scrutiny. When they persisted, she merely told them that she gave several people her name. She did not hide the fact that she provided some private services upon request to some customers, and she had offered her number when asked.

The dead stranger happened to be a narcotics dealer and a wanted criminal, so the paper speculated the death resulting from a drug transaction gone sour. So, they closed that chapter and forgot about him.

It was the other news that shattered the whole district the following week.

The district commissioner Mr. John Karani was transferred to Turkana district in the country's remote part. The paper did not give any reasons for his transfer. It was the routine government transfers, so they said. At first, Tunde ignored the second page of the newspaper. She read on, *in another unrelated matter, the District Commissioner's driver Mr. Juda Tambo has been missing for a week and presumed dead. They discovered a government Land Rover he drove off the road in a flame, and an unrecognizable charred body supposed to be that of the driver was uncovered.* Tunde's jaws dropped and she rushed to the hotel lobby. There were two secret agents waiting at the lobby.

"Are you Tunde?"

"Yes," she hesitated.

"Come with us to the police station."

After preliminary questioning, they released Tunde. She learned that her boss Mr. Giro was put in custody on murder charges. She opened the papers again and read the content. She flipped to the advertisement section, ready to search for another job when another announcement caught her eyes. "Sun hotel and restaurant for sale." She quickly went to a telephone booth and called a number listed. *The property will be auctioned tomorrow.* A hoarse voice told her.

***

A week later.

Sun hotel and restaurant got a new owner and a new name; Tunde renamed the property "Sweet and Sour hotel and restaurant."

After another week, excited Tunde rushed to pick up the phone, "Are you ready to talk with a dead man?" A familiar voice echoed in the distance. She remained silent; she hesitated. "Wrong number." She hung up and waited for five minutes. She then dialed a number in Arusha-Tanzania that she memorized. She could sense the silence on the other end, a sign that she expected. "The dead can't talk," she beamed with a broad smiled.

"I read it in the paper. Congratulations on your new acquisition." Juda praised, before he hung up.

Then she dialed a different number Hassan had given her; a strange person answered.

"A wrong number. We don't have anyone by that name here," replied the voice, as the phone went dead.

"Sweet and Sour," She murmured to herself.

THE DREADFUL CAMP

In the dead silence of the evening before the six o'clock curfew, people hurried and gathered in their huts. Galgallo could hear heavy boots approaching, as people were directing soldiers to his hut. They stopped.

"This is his hut," the guide confirmed, before leaving them in a hurry.

"Galgallo! Toka inge, haraka! Get out." The soldiers propped the hut and kicked it, shouting the orders.

His children started crying.

There was no time to say goodbye to his family. Galgallo glanced at his wife and six children; they huddled together with teary eyes in desperate comfort. Three soldiers with rifles drawn seized Galgallo and threw him to the ground.

They held him down, stepped on him, and struck him with the end of their rifle butt. The soldiers did not talk and did not ask questions but kept beating him.

The old man bled from the nose. He attempted to stand up, but they pushed him down. His fragile weight too much for unruly youthful soldiers. Galgallo looked at them, "Son, why?" The only words he could utter. The soldiers didn't even understand what he was saying, they didn't know his language and they didn't care. He tried to protect his face with his bare hands. The shower of blows on his head and the whole body continued unabated. Galgallo collapsed.

The sharp cry of his wife penetrated the horrendous atmosphere. With a look of terror on their tearful eyes, the children huddled together. The neighbors turned to look towards the direction of the commotion but quickly returned to their huts. Total silence engulfed the area, with only their ears alert to the sounds they waited. No one came to help. Some neighbors peeped their heads out of their huts only to confirm the source of the commotion, before quickly returning to their shelter. Nobody said a word. It wasn't curfew time yet, for the sun had not gone beyond the horizon. The setting sun was the only point of reference for the curfew time.

Silence pervaded the ominous surroundings.

"Hold on. It's enough now. Let's take him." The corporal instructed. They dragged Galgallo through the street for 200 meters to a waiting police Land Rover and threw him behind the back.

One soldier hit him again as Galgallo tried to lift his head. He fell backward with excruciating pain.

In the silence of all these commotions, Marti concentration camp residences would soon observe the six o'clock curfews.

Darmi, Galgallo's wife, held her six children, ages four, six, eight, ten, twelve & fourteen close together. She calmed them. "It'd be all right. He would be safe. We wouldsurvive again." She assured them repeatedly.

Word had already gone around in whispers that the soldiers took Galgallo away. The neighbors waited to wonder who would be next.

Waccu, an elder from Galgallo's clan, calmed down his family. With his hut only at fifteen feet away from Galgallo's hut, he heard the wailing and cries. He waited until the noise had settled and took his steps, surreptitiously one step at a time. He stopped; looking right and left. He had to pass two more rows of huts, and with his back towards the rows of huts, he focused on the narrow path that separated the lines of huts. The dawn to the dusk curfew was in progress, and he can't afford the risk. If caught, he would spend the night in the makeshift prison shelter, and then, the next day would be transferred to the main prison in the town. They will brand him as a shifta or spy. With his eyes on the lookout, Waccu reached Galgallo's hut. He stooped and pushed the thatched framed entrance, calling in a low voice. "It's Waccu, mother of Buna. Untie the door frame and let me in." He sat on the stool, and Darmi started crying. "Don't, and you have to be strong." It was as if they knew it would come to pass. "I don't know who was behind this, but Insha Allah, it will come to pass. We don't know what would happen to the whole community. We might all face the same fate. Only Allah knows how long they will keep us in this Dhaaba" Some community members had already chosen the struggle path, ready to die like men, as they would say. Galgallo's son was among them. Death appeared imminent for the whole community.

The camp was so congested. Huts merely less than 20 meters from each other arranged in rows, dotted the campsite.

Each day people died from hunger or diseases. The number increased daily, and it became a burden to bury the dead. People were so exhausted, that the guards had to force them to bury the dead. An act they would never think of avoiding. The traditional cultural norms of honoring the dead became a thing of the past. The fear of impending calamities lingered on, and every morning, an announcer would call to report the news of the death. The camp's overall sanitary condition was horrible; people used the narrow space between the huts to relieve themselves.

And those who tried to escape and sneaked through the fenced camp, were shot.

***

Two years ago, during the peak of the shifta war of secession, the proud pastoral community members of the whole tribe were forced to move to the vicinity of Marti town and settled in a large, fenced village concentration

199

camp called Dhaaba which means when *everything stopped.*

Each village was allocated a section with records of the number of the people. Galgallo and his village members from Cheraba settled near the gate close to Marti plateau. The fenced camp had four gates guarded by armed home guards. The lines of huts from each village dotted the rugged slope of the Marti plateau. They considered anybody found outside the fence of the camp as a shifta and issued an order "shoot to kill." The "Fagia Shifta, operation's goal of clearing shifta from the area, came into practice. The soldiers committed heinous crimes. They killed, confiscated livestock, and raped women.

A quiet spirit of nationalistic sentiments remained in limbo, with their fate still to be decided. A temporary halt in the way of life for the proud nomadic people became a reality. It was a moment of truth and uncertainty. In one corner of the camp, they enforced different, harsher rules. They demarcated the section with a separate fence and placed extra guards to patrol the perimeter of this segment of the camp. This was where they gathered all the immediate families of those involved in fighting againstthe government of newly independent Kenya. In general, the whole community's fate remained unchanged whether some members were fighting against the government or not. Everyone received cruel treatment. However, the separation of those who had their immediate family members in the shifta movement from the rest was perceived to have had further psychological devastation on innocent family members' morale. The daily constant repression, humiliation, beatings, subjugation, and death threats became a reminder to all people in the camp, and their future marked for demise.

*****

A group of people from northern and northeastern Kenya initiated the so-called "Shifta" war. They wanted to secede from Kenya to Somalia after Kenya got independence. Galgallo and many other people in the region cherished the idea of secession from the newly independent Kenya to join the Republic of Somalia with people of a similar religious background. It was a community decision, and unfortunately, they never considered the merits of the findings and the consequences. Galgallo remembered all the incidents that led to the war. At first, the elders from his area were against the idea because most of his tribal members do not live in Somalia. The issue of cultural similarity and religious affiliation with Somali people appeared plausible to most of them. Galgallo plunged into action and recruited several people, including his brother and a son. It took a while for him and others to realize the debacle of their judgment, but he did not regret the actions he took.

***

Home guards guarded Marti village concentration camp day and night; observing the movements of the local people closely.

Through its informers and chief, the government knew each family member who was on the side of shifta. The word shifta was associated with banditry, although to Galgallo and others like him, the shifta war was a war of liberation. The tribe members had to decide whether to remain with Kenya or secede. Like many community decisions, when the elders of the tribe decided, the whole population followed. Individual members of the tribe may not have embraced the idea; however, they did not complain if people were not satisfied. The young and healthy men were called upon to join the fighting force. They went to Somalia for training and infiltrated back into Kenya and fought against the government soldiers. Those who could not participate in the

201

actual fighting volunteered and offered their sons, brothers, cousins, and nephews for the cause.

The whole community was then moved to one location and settled. Each village elder was made accountable for the members of his village.

The nomadic tribe depended on livestock for their survival. Galgallo questioned the rationale the government used and how they would expect them to live without their animals. He was known for expressing his views openly, and as a tribal elder, everybody respected his opinions.

Galgallo disagreed with the rules handed over to the chief, with specific guidelines that everybody should settle their animals near the village concentration camp. They wanted only one or two members of the family to take care of the animals. He considered the rules imposed unfair and unrealistic for their situations. In particular, the animals' restrictions to the 10-square mile radius were a ridiculous and laughable notion that anybody with a rational mind could not accept. But the chief received instructions to enforce the rule, and they decreed that the army would confiscate any animal found beyond the designated 10-mile radius. Abiding by this rule was impossible. There was not enough grass for the animals within the specified area. The animals that roamed beyond were confiscated, and the ones that remained, died of hunger and disease; there was no grass for them to feed.

***

"I know he's guilty. Keep him away. He broke the 10-mile radius rule for grazing, and he opposed the dawn to dusk curfews. He's behind all the problems that have happened. His son is among the bandits that ambushed the army lorry last month and killed several soldiers. He knows their whereabouts, and we should not let him out soon," reported Chief Godana.

The Inspector concluded the interview. He read through all the statements in the report on Galgallo and made sure that what the chief said about him was fully documented. But as he looked through again, the comments didn't add up nicely. Galgallo didn't deny that he supported the war on the side of shifta. The whole community was behind the war, and he acknowledged that fact to the Inspector, but the real reason, according to Galgallo, was the personal animosity between him and the chief, not because of Galgallo's support for shifta cause.

"Anything else?"

"No, sir, but Galgallo is a real danger." The chief repeated.

Inspector Mambo had been in the area long enough, and he knew the strength of the bandits. He had already planted his informers within the group and understood the idea of concentration camps worked well. The Inspector knew what some people were capable of and who he needed to watch.

He had learned enough about Galgallo from his other informers. He had no doubt in his mind that a person like Galgallo could easily convince the members of his tribe. *It would've been nice to have a person with that kind of caliber on your side during the time of war, but on the other hand, you have to respect your opponent's views as well,* he thought. This was a question of power and subjugation. How would these people dare to try and oppose the authority of the ruling government? The government had just won independence from Great Britain. The country won through the hardship and long, devastating war of liberation where several Kenyans died. Inspector Mambo was irritated by the shifta war and considered it a nuisance and an inconvenience. He even called it the stupid war initiated by ignorant people who deserved to be punished and destroyed.

At one time, he thought of carrying out an outrageous and wicked plan. For him, the easiest way to shortening this war was to poison the river they depended on, and that would have ended the problem altogether. Inspector Mambo was not new to wars; he knew the real war fought by his tribe. Some of his closest relatives suffered the consequence of Kenya's actual liberation war that won the government's independence in 1963.

Inspector Mambo often said. *"And then all hell broke loose when these misguided people carved out a chunk of land and decided to secede to Somalia."*

He even knew their closely guarded secrets; he couldn't believe that some of these people still wanted the British to continue their rule. The British government had put them into the privileged group-second class citizen with Asians. And yet the same British colonist betrayed them before they left. They failed to implement the referendum they promised. Sometimes he wondered whether these nomadic people were part of this country. Before he came to Marti, inspector Mambo served in another town in Northern Kenya; and there, he implemented most of his crazy ideas, including beatings and all forms of torture. His favorite method was to burn the culprits' nail with the tip of smoking cigarettes and keep them naked on the cold cemented floor. By his admission, he thought this cruel, sadistic method worked.

The interpreter looked up at Galgallo, trying to search for suitable words to say. He couldn't possibly translate the word Galgallo was telling him. Inspector Mambo looked from one to another. "What did he say?"

"Just a minute, sir, I have to elaborate to him," Galgallo spoke only the local language dialect (Booran). "I wanted him to understand your questions fully." The Inspector waited as the interpreter and Galgallo conversed. It appeared that Galgallo was insisting and kept repeating the word Allah, which Inspector Mambo knew, and then added.

"Naam cuuf waaqaat tissa, yoo guuyaan gaae, waani dhoowaan hinjirtu,"

"This is what Galgallo said. *Tell him that Allah will protect everyone, and if the final day comes nothing will prevent it.* God gives lives and takes it away," said Galgallo. The interpreter, looking from Galgallo to the Inspector hesitated, and talked with Galgallo again.

"Are you out of your mind? You better start planning how you'd save your life. You're talking to a non-believer about your God whom he would not recognize. I don't know how to tell him this."

Inspector Mambo became a little impatient at the exchange of words he couldn't possibly understand. It seemed Galgallo had few words, but the interpreter kept talking and talking as if he was convincing Galgallo. After a pause, he demanded. "What did he say?"

"He said, Allah was his witness that he did not feed the rebels. The rebels came and took his animal by force and slaughtered. He also reiterated and confirmed that his son was in Somalia but did not know the location."

But the Inspector insisted that his son was in Kenya, and he knew it. The interpreter again looked at Galgallo. He spoke to him and emphasized that the best thing for him to do, was to look for answers that would satisfy the Inspector and save himself. It was apparent that some of the local dialect words were not easy to translate. The translator wanted to help Galgallo, so he substituted some harsh words Galgallo used for some suitable and compromising statements. For instance, Galgallo wanted the Inspector to lift the 10-mile radius restrictions and allow the community's elders to make decisions that concerned the tribe. The interpreter softened the words in the translation of language and told the Inspector a different thing.

"Sir, Galgallo is sorry for the mistakes he made in the past. He says that he simply requested the chief to pass on the word to you that the animals have depleted the grass in the assigned area. They needed the restrictions lifted and requested you to extend the area the animals would cover; otherwise, they would all die. The animals would not survive without grass."

The interpreter hesitated, casting a glance at Galgallo, before continuing.

"The other thing about his son, he had already told you, and he did not know at all."

Galgallo had another request; the guards blocked him from conducting his prayers. And he wanted them instructed not to interfere and lift this restriction.

But the interpreter did not translate that and instead told the Inspector that Galgallo wanted to have warm water in the morning, to brush and wash face if possible.

The Inspector looked unconvinced.

Galgallo remained in detention, and they kept him in a tiny cell room at the back of the police living quarters. The small room initially served as a waiting room but was after converted into a prison cell. They never intended to hold people there for a long time. Galgallo was kept handcuffed during the night, but they removed his handcuff during the day, although he remained in his room. Occasionally, they would allow him to come out into the sun but only for a limited time. The guards were there all the time, guarding the whole premises. For the first few weeks, even relatives were not allowed to see him.

The only time he saw people he knew was when he ate food, but the woman who brought him food from the local restaurant was told not to talk with him. She had acontract with the government to provide food for the prisoners. She would come to the guard, test her food in the presence of a guard, wait for about 10 minutes, and then take the meal to the prisoner. That day the guard told the woman to carry the food to Galgallo. As she delivered the food, she mentioned only one word in the local language, and Galgallo did not need further explanation. He pushed the food aside. The guard grabbed the woman and pulled her into the office.

"What did you tell him?" He demanded. She understood Swahili and told the guard that she greeted the elder in her mother tongue. "What else? Why is he suddenly withdrawing?"

He wondered what would have made Galgallo shed tears. He never saw tears in his eyes even when four soldiers beat him. "What kind of word made him weep?" He demanded an explanation.

The woman trembled. She had broken the rule. She was sure to lose her contract with the police, and they would brand her as a supporter as well, but she had to tell the guard what she said to him. "It's about his son. I told him." She said with a trembling voice. The guard looked at her elegant, youthful beauty. She bowed her head down. "I'm sorry," she pleaded.

The members of the police force had also committed all kinds of atrocities against the local innocent people. Overwhelmed by fear of persecution, some of the local people who questioned the authorities as Galgallo had, found themselves on the wrong side. It was a time when no human rights ever existed in the land.

Galgallo gnawed his teeth. He'd promised himself never to show and succumb to any emotions. He'd lost a brother in the war and now his elder son. He also learned that the army had confiscated his animals. They're now leaving him destitute. *If only he could get out of this*, he conjured a dark plan; *he would strangle Godana and squeeze the last drop of breath out of him with his bare hands*. The intensity of his thought process would even push him beyond the traditional rules of law. No member of his tribe would kill another member of the tribe. This was the rule of law that he was made to believe and abide by, but Galgallo was sure to break that law when he got out. He had to punish Godana for what he put him and his family through, but his faith in God and religion would not allow him to follow that revengeful path. He lay on his back and contemplated what he would do next. *If it is the will of Allah, I had to accept it*. He murmured to himself.

***

Galgallo languished in the filthy cell.

Outside, the oppressive life continued.

Several months later, the Inspector had another meeting with Galgallo.

"Tell him exactly what I'm going to say. Find the exact word. I'll be brief," the Inspector beamed. He looked at Galgallo again. His demeanor had not changed at all, and it'd been six months.

"Tell him that he is free to go for now. Tell him and emphasize that I have spared his life, but I would shoot him if he ever broke the law again. Tell him that if that happens, I will drag his corpse into the street for everyone to see as an example of what would happen to bandits. Then throw his dead body outside in the bush for hyenas to feast on. He will not receive a proper burial and would remain an example to others like him. I will do it. I swear, I will." The Inspector hesitated as he wondered why he should threaten this powerless man. He knew the war was almost over, and there was nothing Galgallo could do.

But Galgallo kept silent. He lifted his eyes and looked at the Inspector in the eyes. "Tell him that only God could save him and if it were the will of Allah, it would happen, no matter what he says. Tell him that I am not afraid of death."

The interpreter mumbled. It was not the words he'd expected, but he had to do something to make this translation less confrontational, smooth, and peaceful.

"Sir, as you might have noticed, this man is very religious. He said that Allah knows the truth, and he was thankful that God guided your decisions in the right direction. He said that he is a law-abiding innocent citizen." It was not the exact translation, but the translator thought it was the closest he could do. He thought that further argument would worsen the situation for Galgallo

"Let me not see you again." The Inspector warned.

Chief Godana took the news of Galgallo's release with bitterness. He had doubts about the wrong actions he took against him. The clan members had already pleaded with him for his release, but Godana refused. He thought he could convince the Inspector to keep him long in the cell or even get rid of him if possible. However, the Inspector made his decisions without consulting him. Godana wondered whether the Inspector knew the real reason behind his insistence in keeping Galgallo locked away. Probably some of his clan members might have guessed the long animosity between them.

Galgallo, for sure, knew why Godana had caused him all these problems. It was not because he was outspoken about the injustice committed by government soldiers. It was not because the chief failed to prevent the problems directed to the community in general. The chief had little control over what happened during the war. He was a mere instrument, a means by which the government machinery operated and directed the war. The real issue with him and Godana stemmed from ways back during the days of their youthful years.

It was a regrettable event, and Galgallo looked back with shame about why the community had accepted such behavior. He came to realize late in life after he accepted the Islamic faith that some of what his age-mates and tribal members did during those years were wrong, especially the habits of keeping mistresses outside marriage. There was nothing he could do to change what happened in the past. The sins of his past behavior still haunted him. He was not ready to tell Godana to forget the past. They had never talked to each other face to face after the incident. Galgallo admitted that he wronged him, and he attributed his foolishness to a hasty youthful decision based on lust, and Godana didn't forgive him.

After all these years, Galgallo could still remember the incident vividly. The kidnap of Godana's bride one week before the wedding was the most humiliating event, and the tribe even named the season after the event.

"The season of the kidnap of Godana's bride." The incident that Galgallo caused divided the tribe, and he accepted the fine and moved on with his newly acquired wife, but the hatred that Godana showed lingered on, and he was ready to revenge. He got the opportunity to revisit the past and crush him in body and spirit. He now had the upper hand, and the shifta war gave him the cover he needed to implement his plans. He would like to see Galgallo destitute and reduced to poverty and humiliation. Chief Godana was behind everything that happened to Galgallo and his animals. The tribal members knew this long feud had caused divisions, and while they acknowledged what Galgallo did in the past was wrong, they strongly condemned Chief Godana's revenge during the term of strife that inflicted the whole community.

***

Galgallo brooded over the bleak future ahead of him as he approached the gate. He was more concerned about his own children's future. Without animals, he would not make it, and since the only trade he knew was herding cattle, he didn't know what else to do. The home guard allowed him in.

One after another, he recounted the events that happened during his long absence from home. The army had killed so many people he knew, and those who did not die at the hands of government soldiers, had not survived the epidemic diseases that engulfed the camp. Galgallo listened as his wife narrated to him all that happened. It seemed like so many years had passed. That night he slept little. Thanks to Allah, he offered a silent prayer. He was glad that his clan members fooled the army when they came to look for Galgallo's animals. The ingenuity of the clan members' plan saved most of his cattle. They took some of his cows and mixed with their own to mislead the army and the chief.

A day after his release, a clan member, elder Waccu, and several members from his clan came to visit him as they often did when Galgallo was in detention. Darmi couldn't help overhearing what they conversed in whispers. The first clan member left with two of his sons, then soon another clan member left with two more children. Darmi, Galgallo's wife, left her hut with the last two young kids. She left her shelter as if she was just visiting a neighbor. The guard did not notice. She joined her children later, three miles away from the camp. Elder Waccu also stepped out with two of Galgallo's kids as if he was strolling just with kids as he usually did. He walked past the guard unnoticed. Before six o'clock curfew, people could get out of the camp and visit bushes on the camp's edge to collect firewood.

Galgallo followed them later. He was alone. One after another, the whole day after about two hours, his family sneaked out of the camp. The home guard changed each other after intervals of two hours. Galgallo was the last to leave the camp gate, but he used a different exit. They planned to meet each other at a prearranged site near the thick bush three miles away from the guards' prying eyes. When all the family members arrived at their destination, Galgallo looked at the camp once more.

"No more," he whispered.

His wife covered the mouth of her little child about to cry. "Shush, no! no!" The child seemed to understand the strange request; despite the hunger that kept him awake, the child remained silent, but it was only for a while.

"We had to leave now before anybody noticed us," Galgallo told his wife. Up to that time, she did not ask where they were going. She knew in her heart that they were about to make a long-distance journey.

"But where are we going?" She finally decided to ask, just in case her intuitions failed her.

Galgallo kept quiet for what seemed to be a long time.

"Not now, it would be a while before we see each other. Take care of the children. Anywhere would be better than this place," He said.

"What?"

He held his hand against her mouth. "No. Go with the children. Waccu and some of the clan members will guide you. I will join you later. Go. You can go with them."

"Where?" she attempted to ask again.

Galgallo called his fourteen-year-old son aside. "Help your mother and take care of your brothers and sisters. I'll meet all of you there. It's not safe for all of us to be together before we crossed the border to Somalia. They would track me down. I will use a different route." He kissed him on the forehead.

The short emotional moments ended abruptly. "No tears, we are alive," Galgallo assured the children and his wife.

Darmi stood gazing after him. "How sure are you that we will be safe there? Here at least we have all our other families." She sobbed.

"Hold yourself together. We will be safe. We will have our freedom to move around. God's willing, after the end of the war, we will be home again. I promise." He paused. "As our elders would say, 'Fulaa keesaa dhufan beekan malee, fulaa itti deeman hin beekan'. *A person will only know where he came from. He doesn't know where he's going.* You're right. We will never know the future, but we knew what we had gone through already."

Elder Waccu led them through a winding footpath. He'd planned each step; they had to walk the whole night and hide and sleep during the day.

Galgallo looked at them as they moved away. "I will see you. Insha Allah," he offered his silent invocation to his almighty.

He looked once more towards the direction of the camp. A weary look on his face depicted all. He had grown old, and whatever fate awaited him in the foreign land, he would embrace it with faith. He had to trust this new venture. Galgallo once more looked towards the Marti plateau still visible to the naked eye.

He turned towards the east to begin a long journey of many days, filled with uncertainty. The perils of the wild animals and the enemy he was running away from, was still ahead of him. But had no time for regrets; it was a bold decision, a hope of new life that he had to live with in the future.

THE UNFORTUNATE Event

THE UNFORTUNATE EVENT

Halkano walked over to the other side of the Land Rover, where his elder daughter sat.

"You know what to do," he told her.

"But daddy, Khadija doesn't listen to me."

"Khadija! Do everything your sister says," he instructed, as he patted her on the head.

All five children would stay with their grandmother in the village.

"Khadija has a mind of her own. She's not afraid to try new things. I hope she does the right thing." Halkano acknowledged.

"I don't know how they would behave without me being there. Maybe it's not a good idea."

"Come on, the children have been in the village before, and they liked it. They'll be fine," countered Halkano, as he tried to convince his wife.

Even the driver had said the same thing to Rukia: *The kids would enjoy and have fun in the village.*

"Besides," he continued. "I have to win this election, and you have to be in town to help until after the election. Grandma also insisted that the kids be with her during the vacation. She was shocked to hear that our youngest daughter never saw a real cow, and she planned to introduce them to the real culture. And, in any case," he emphasized. "Grandma has the final say, and she insisted that the children should go to the village. I support her decision. She would take good care of them."

Rukia hesitated, but Halkano tugged her gently along.

"Stop worrying, and let's get moving. The meeting will start soon."

Halkano led his wife and some of his supporters to the meeting, where he was about to deliver his campaign speech.

Halkano Galmo felt agitated; the crowd surged with each word he uttered. During the last two campaign speeches, he'd deliberately avoided the issue of girls' circumcision. Not that he agreed with this barbaric act, as he regarded it a violation of human rights. But as the election came closer, he felt the urge to tell the people to stop this act of humiliation. Halkano understood the sensitivity of this topic. The government had banned this practice many years ago, but his people still circumcised young girls in remote villages. You wouldn't hear people talk about it in the open or in towns. You wouldn't hear the cry from the pain inflicted by the crooked razor used for slicing and chopping off the floppy tongue-like flesh out of the little girls' treasured cache. The innocent little ones grew up in the tradition that allowed these practices. Their mothers were circumcised, as were their grandmothers and great-grandmothers.

"We don't have even a proper word for this thing we practice." Halkano buzzed into the loudspeaker. "We use words like, *qabanqaba, guur urra,*" Halkano had difficulty translating the word into any other languages he knows. He spoke in the local dialect. For the benefits of those who do not understand his native tongue, he switched to the National language-Kiswahili and delivered his political speeches. His translator had difficulty translating the two words used for circumcision-Guur urra (pierce the ear), a term used metaphorically. The simplest he could come up with was a direct translation of the words, and many people in the audience who did not understand the native language laughed. The crowd murmured, and somebody shouted what he meant in Kiswahili as *kutahiri*. Halkano calmed the audience and resumed. "Yes, you all know the dirty little secret we harbored for a long time. It is time that we let the secret out and bury it. Your elected member," here the audience turned towards the incumbent Member of Parliament Honorable Molu Iya, who sat in the front row seat waiting for his turn to address the public. "You sent him to the parliament for the last fifteen years, he knew the practice existed, and his daughter is probably circumcised." People booed him for that cruel embarrassing statement, but Halkano understood the nature of politics. The politicians do anything to win their case, even if it meant reducing his opponent to the ground, he would do it, but he promised to stick to the facts.

Halkano watched the reactions of the people. Some of the young, educated women felt embarrassed; he could see it on their faces. Halkano had refrained from attacking his opponents, but Honorable Molu would not spare him, and would probably tear him down when his turn came. During the last campaign speeches, Halkano focused only on what he could do for the people if elected, while his opponent, honorable Molu spent the whole one-hour of his address, attacking him. He smeared him with all kinds of scandalous unsubstantiated rumors.

It was as if suddenly the people discovered the horrible loss, and Halkano's speech exposed their nakedness. He'd begrudgingly stated the fact and didn't want to open the wound. They all bore the mark of their hidden scar, shielded from the outside world. He would never understand how they felt. He gazed at the pretty faces with a reassuring smile. *Or maybe they don't miss anything. How can you miss what you don't have?* He thought.

"I know I shouldn't have opened this topic." Halkano continued. "Those of you who had the unfortunate experience, please understand. I'm not here to denigrate all our past cultural practices. It was not your fault, so don't feel guilty about it now. As a community, we can all take responsibility for this horrible mistake." He paused to let his words sink. "Let's stop this act now." He looked towards the direction where women sat. "Think of your little girls. Don't let anybody rob your little angels of God's beautiful creation. It was wrong then, and it's wrong now for us to watch and subject our innocent and vulnerable membersof society to this cruel act, in the name of tradition." The silent audiences looked on. It was not the usual ululation with thumping and clapping of hands; only a few people clapped.

Later that evening, Halkano met with some of his supporters. They generally gave him high points for his speeches; however, they did not like his choice on circumcision. They felt ashamed. Many of them believed that he shouldn't have taken this as a campaign issue at all. They considered cultural issues as something that should die by itself. Some of his women supporters also felt the same way. Halkano wondered why everybody feared to talk about the thing they know and considered wrong, in public.

At midnight, supporters still thronged his place; some of them just wanted to be seen, and others had formed a habit of just hanging around. When finally, everybody left his residence, Halkano reflected on what had happened. As usual, he consulted his wife and wanted to find out what she thought. Rukia was not rather keen to talk about circumcision. She felt the timing was not right, and as a master strategist, Halkano, often relied on her for ideas. She took an unpaid vacation from her counseling position, just to help him with the campaign and the paperwork.

"I'm a hundred percent behind you in everything you do. It's a little too fast for people to grasp. Yes, as you mentioned, most of us feel bad; now the whole world knows that we're still practicing girls' circumcision. You know I told you already that I would not like to give birth again just because of the humiliation I would face during childbirth. I do not want those nurses to look at my body with strange expressions on their faces."

He glanced at her. "Dear, there is nothing to be ashamed of now. It was not your fault. You're adorable, intelligent, and a dream of a wife to have" He consoled her.

"Thank you." She paused. "Ya, it's easy for you to say that my dear husband." He remembered she mentioned to him how she felt, and he knew there was nothing he could do to help her situation, but at the same time, *somebody had to face this gigantic cultural enigma*. He thought.

Circumcision was a word that only existed in the back of her mind. Rukia heard all that the nurses said about her anatomy at the time when she gave birth. She understood their language. She learned the Meru language when her father was administrative police, stationed in Meru town. The woman who helped in her delivery seemed to take pride in retelling the different types of circumcisions practiced. To Rukia, it was all the same. The practice robbed her of the irreplaceable treasure, her natural gift. The essence of her femininity. *What difference did it make? All circumcisions are the same and included the removal of all the parts of the external genitalia.* In this type of circumcision, known as infibulation, they'd remove the inner fleshy part of the organ and stitch the large lips' edges together. Some tribes used thorns for stitching and allowed it to heal by restraining the movement of the girls. Their legs tied together for several weeks to heal the wound. The nurse took tremendous pleasure in telling the story about what she saw in some parts of Northern Kenya, Somalia, and Sudan. Rukia twisted her head in disgust. She was sure the circumcision they practiced in her area was limited only to removing the little tongue like flesh and the outer part. They did not use thorns to sew her body. *That never happened, and in any case, it would never happen to her children.* She believed the backward practice had ended with her generation.

Rukia paused. "In any case, a jail term you suggested for the person who conducted the act was a little too harsh. Do you know that there was a reporter in the audience?"

"What are you getting at!" Halkano turned to his wife, and he saw it in her eyes. "You want me to keep silent about this? I thought you should be at the forefront of this issue."

"Yes, but my approach would be a little different. I will empower girls with education. Education is the key to unlock and clear this stigma. Our religion doesn't support this act. They are not many people who would support this practice today. It will die out."

"I heard that there are still some people who practice it. I don't know how else we could stop it. We are in a different era now, sure, but unless we jolt them with severe punishment, it will not end." Halkano took a deep breath and resumed. "This is the 21st century. Circumcision is a crime. It must stop. I will not change my stance."

His wife tilted her head. He noticed a little anger in her words. "You know I'm a strong advocate for the eradication of this act, but I think the best method, as I said, is through education and enforcing the laws. Banning the act was good, but it did not help stop the action. People do it in the villages. Some of them even send their daughters to the villages to continue the practice."

"What?"

"What, you mean you don't know?" she asked.

Halkano stopped. *I hope that doesn't give my mother any weird ideas*, he thought.

"Yes, education is the key, but circumcisions take place before they even start school."

Halkano had argued with his wife about this topic before. He knew her stand. She saw the root cause of the problem was the lack of equality for women. At one time, she accused him of not doing anything rather than talk, but when he meant doing something, like suggesting a jail term for the perpetrators of this act, his wife turned cold.

He shrugged and changed the topic.

***

Halkano's supporters had started calling him "Honorable Member," a title reserved for elected members of parliament. As a favorite candidate for the upcoming parliamentary election, Halkano had everything in place to win the election. Education, wealth, influential clan supporters, and personal charisma. He'd laid out plans for community development and had completed discussions with the team at the provincial office. Later that day, he met with nonprofit organizations to follow up on his earlier request on special projects dear to his heart. *We have neglected women and girls, and if elected, I am determined to do something to uplift them.*

The bulk of his supporters included women. The group of women supporters requested him to consider their unique situation that every politician seemed to ignore after being elected. Halkano looked at the community issues with an open mind. He understood that the lack of educational opportunities for girls was a real problem. Deep inside his guts, he knew what he wanted to do was the right thing for his community. Halkano was not the usual breed of politician. He had not been tainted by clan politics, and for sure, he hoped to get some votes from tribes other than his own.

Regardless of how things would turn out, he promised the people that he would fight for them and restore their dignity. His primary goal was to unite the people contrary to what others thought about his controversial stand on some issues. He always focused on the best interests of his community.

The next day was busy. Halkano returned to the hotel to finish some of the paperwork. He went through the rough speech notes, put some ideas that he would forward to the people. Judging from the reaction during the last three campaign speeches, the crowd exalted his ideas. Next week he would conduct his final campaign rally and then wait for one more week, and then the whole drama would be over. He envisioned the smile on his face and couldn't wait tosee the reactions of his supporters thronging the street with joy and song of praise. He would expect them to carry him on their shoulders, singing and feasting in honor of the grand occasion. He would then give a press conference and outline his programs for the next five years. His supporters would continue with the celebration throughout the week.

Halkano met with some of his supporters, and they went over the campaign plans again, making sure that he left out nothing. He learned that his opponent had started his dirty tricks. It had become difficult to dislodge his opponent, who was known to use all manner of political maneuvers tactics against anybody who tried to oppose him. For the last three elections, Molu Iya held to the seat, not because of what he did for the people but because everybody feared to oppose him. Every time opponents garnered the strength to topple him, something was sure to happen to them. In the last couple of elections, his opponents blamed him for buying voting cards from the electors and destroying them. They even accused him of hiring thugs to ambush the villages where he was not likely to get support. In rural areas, people did not prioritize elections. They busied with their own lives catering to their immediate needs.

While some of the activities attributed to his opponent were illegal and never condoned, Molu used them anyway. He had the support of some corrupt influential government officials he'd already bribed to carry out his dirty work. In the remote part of the country where most of his people lived, little had changed. One of the issues that Molu failed to eradicate was the lawless state of anarchy dominated by tribal clashes. The rumors circulating among the local people implicated him as the main instigator. The perpetrators were on his payroll so, they rumored. They struck with impunity and without regard for human lives. The thugs took property, but some of them burnt down villages and killed men and raped women causing terrible carnage.

The momentum of the coming election had caught everybody off guard. People were spreading all sorts of rumors, innuendo, backbiting, or backstabbing techniques played there and here. Some people played their cards very well and learned how to take advantage of the situation. They promised both candidates and got something from each politician. Some adamant ones stuck to their supporters and publicly denounced the other candidates. Halkano's opponent had established government machinery behind him, and his followers had caused havoc in some villages. They barred Halkano from entering one village. Halkano's fans blamed the chief of the location, who harassed them and blocked them from talking with people. In a system where there was no fair election, and voters' lists were practically inaccessible to the opponents, Halkano's supporters only hoped for the best. They expected massive rigging by the incumbent, but they were ready to fight to the end. In the previous election five years ago, voting papers for more than the number of the people in the region surfaced, and they were all marked for Molu Iya. How he got all those votes remained a mystery, and yet he was declared a winner.

The report from Kula location and in the village where Halkano's mother lived did not look impressive. Halkano had confidence that he would get enough support from the people who resided in towns, especially young people and women. However, one would never know the outcome of elections. The experience of the past polls revealed that the town people were not reliable. They could easily be convinced, and the more you bribe, the more likely you would get their votes. Halkano knew some people had sold their voting cards, and then there were people who planned to vote for both candidates. They promised to vote for several candidates, but they would always decide to pick only one of them on Election Day. Unlike the inflexibility of the town people, the village inhabitants would typically remain committed. If they promised to vote for oneperson, they would likely do so, and no money would change their minds. Winning the rural people's confidence had become center stage and a pivotal base that any politician loved to grab. People believed that the incumbent would have an advantage over the newcomer. Honorable Molu appeared to have established his base regarding the rural people, where his supporters kept instilling fear into illiterate innocent people's minds.

"How are we doing?" Halkano's voice was barely audible, exhausted from talking with people during door-to-door campaign. He sat down to check the final detail with his campaign adviser Baraka. "So far, everything's going on well. We'll call some of the business owners. "Baraka confirmed. "The report coming from different locations were positive Honorable, but remember we have to wait one more week, and anything can change the votes and the total outcome of the election," Baraka added.

"I can sense the mood. Things are looking promising, what do you think?"

"I think we will win big this time. The era of Molu is over."

"I noticed a missed call from my wife."

"Oh, she called the office, and she's on the way, and the feedback she is getting is also promising. It was a good idea to send her to your in-laws. Your brother-in-law is influential in that area."

"Just relax, Honorable Halkano," Baraka whispered. "Let's have a "*nyama choma*" roast beef for lunch. The future is near, and we need big plans." The group moved to their favorite restaurant. Most of Halkano's supporters ate at Gada restaurant. He had one section of the room permanently reserved for him. The waiters knew what he wanted, and he couldn't wait to eat roasted goat ribs.

The manager of the restaurant approached Halkano and whispered something into his ears. Halkano jacked his head and stopped eating. "It's a call from your wife. She was trying to reach you, and it is very urgent. She wants to speak with you."

Halkano took the phone," What? No! No! Why? Why? It can't be right! How could this have happened? Why did you allow it!"

His supporters looked at each other. They couldn't know what could have caused that sudden terrible reaction in Halkano. One of his followers grabbed the manager by his shirt's collar, demanding to know what was happening.

"Why? Why?" that was the only word they could hear him say.

Halkano left quickly without telling anybody what happened. The supporters by then could only guess the news he received must be sad. Some speculated that one of his family members might've died, or something worse happened to them. Even his driver precisely could not say what happened. His boss just told him to drive to Kula that night.

The five-hour drive in the Toyota Land Cruiserseemed like an endless journey. The rugged road and the terrain of the forgotten North fueled his already boiled moods. Except for the frequent cursing of the road conditions, Halkano sat with an absent mind. He still couldn't believe that his mother would do something like that.

The sun was about to set when Halkano arrived. People in the little town had a habit of stopping the vehicles before they reached their destination. As soon as they identified Halkano's Toyota, his supporters wanted to talk with him, but Halkano instructed his driver not to stop until he reached his home, where his wife and the children stayed. Earlier on, his wife told him she had the children with her at their house. A small house Halkano bought in the town the previous year when his opponent accused him of being a stranger who did not have a home in the area. From the time he declared to stand for election, Halkano made sure he had a place to live when he visited his hometown. He promised his supporters that he would come home to stay. Halkano didn't have the mood to see anybody else, but people converged into his residence. The campaign atmosphere was in high gear, and his supporters didn't waste any time. They were feasting even before the election victory. They had confidence that they would win. Everybody seemed to act normal as if nothing happened. Inevitably, nothing significant happened, and people even didn't consider the incident with Halkano's daughter as newsworthy.

"She'll be fine. There was no infection." His wife said.

"Did you have her arrested? As I instructed."

"How could I do that? She's your mother."

"She would pay for this crime. And you too, it's your responsibility. How could this happen while you're around?"

"I was not there when she did it. I would not have allowed, you know that" his wife sobbed.

"It's over, and you have to leave." He ordered.

Halkano went to a police station to report the incident; they sent for his mother.

The next day the whole town stood still. People whispered." Did you hear what Halkano did? Unbelievable! How could he send his mother to jail? His mother! He ordered her arrested, and she's in a tiny cell now?" They spread the news, and at each corner, people gathered to exchange the information with twist and flavor to fit their political narratives. His political opponents, thrilled with this unexpected gift, rushed to define and predict what Halkano could do if elected. They painted a gloomy picture of what Halkano was capable of and how the whole community would be in danger if he got to power. By word of mouth, whispers in the bedrooms, and by telephone, they fanned the news through the villages. In all the gatherings, the first opening word was, *did you hear the news?*

Halkano's supporters murmured in silence. A dense cloud of doubts had set in their minds. One or two staunch followers had to face him, but they too thought he'd gone crazy. The old members of his clan consulted each other and held an immediate meeting.

Halkano sat and waited. "Why do you want to talk with me? "he demanded to know.

Mzee Tari cleared his voice. "Son, you have committed an abominable act. I've never seen anything like what you did in all the 80 years that I have lived, as our elders would say. " *Arbi xiira ufii hin dhadhabu, jedhani*-An elephant doesn't get tired of his weight."

He waited. Halkano did not speak.

"Release your mother now. We're ready to declare that the order didn't come from you, and it was a mistake."

Halkano sat in bewilderment. He thought about how *they'd turned him into a culprit now.* They didn't even mention his daughter, and for them, what his mother did was a traditional practice. *Just a regular thing*, it's our tradition, they said. Right then, he knew he was fighting a losing battle. A battle that would be a reminder to him and all those who would like to change things.

Why was circumcision of girls necessary? Nobody could tell him why. He checked the religious book and couldn't find any recommendations for girls. The practice was just an archaic tradition that failed to die, and he would kill it, but contrary to what he thought, it brought him down. After the elders left, Mzee Tari turned to Halkano.

"Hold your family together. You still have time to mend what you broke. Your mother did what she knew to do within the traditional parameters. She would not last long. I understand she hasn't eaten for the last two days. Don't allow her to die in jail. You'll never recover from the doom, and this would be a reminder to your legacy, as long as this generation remembers what you did. They would never elect you." He shook his head.

Again, Halkano didn't respond. Mzee Tari then continued. "Your wife. Take her back. You need her. You don't divorce in anger. An angry mind is irrational, and it is against our tradition to divorce anyway. Besides, she didn't commit any crime." He added.

Halkano looked at the older man squarely. Outside Halkano's residence, the news remained tense. People no longer talked about elections anymore. The focus was on his mother's deteriorating health.

It'd been two days since the last time she saw the light of the sun. In the meantime, Halkano's opponents worked day and night. They had the opportunity to turn things around. They twisted and switched their slogans, and by word of mouth spread their news. Their motto said it all. *Somebody who could take his mother to jail will stop at nothing.* The opponents then spread rumors that his mother had died in prison. There was no truth to what they said, but people believed in everything in rural areas where they passed news by word of mouth. The story about his mother in jail had already gone beyond the region to other parts of the regions where other tribal members lived, including southern Ethiopia. From now on, they would remember him as the terrible son who put his mother in jail to die. No matter how much Halkano wanted to set an example, the community wasn't receptive to this punishment, if they didn't believe it fitted the crime. Not a single person questioned or even asked how his daughter was doing. They would never consider what his mother did as a crime; in their eyes, his mother only did what culture and traditions glorified and practiced for all these years.

Halkano wondered why his supporters, who had crisscross rivers and forests to campaign and extol his virtues hadn't said a word about what happened to his daughter. Their only concern was how he mistreated his mother. One or two of his loyal members suggested that his political opponent had a hand in this matter. He was willing to implicate Halkano's political opponents as culprits and the people behind the incident. Halkano refused to allow that to happen. "We have to do the right thing. It doesn't matter anymore." He murmured to himself.

Looking back at all the events of the past few days, Halkano realized his error in judgment.

He'd failed to educate his children and explain what he didn't like in the culture that he tried to bring them up. He didn't prepare them for the incident that happened. He never expected what happened and the idea that he had to deal with it at a personal level. The question of circumcision of his girls never propped up because he knew that would never happen, and yet part of his life, the life in which he grew up, the culture that he loved and cherished, failed to recognize the wrong. He stood alone. He was partly to blame. His mother did what she knew how to do out of ignorance when judged from his point of view. She did not feel guilty. *How can she feel guilty when she knew for sure that what she did was a good part of what her culture endorsed?* Halkano remained perplexed. He now believed the danger that such a group mentality could pose.

Earlier on, when he asked his daughter Khadija why she didn't refuse, she replied that the other girls and her grandmother told her that she would be ridiculed in the future and would never be married or bear children of her own. Halkano shook his head with tears. "No, honey. I'm sorry I failed you." He wiped the tears off quickly. It never occurred to him that unfortunate event like what happened could happen to him. He realized how vulnerable he'd been, and for the first time in his life, Halkano felt isolated, but he had to face the truth. He recalled the traditional proverb.
Iltii waan garte sodaatti, gurri waan dhaagaaye sodaata. Theeyefears what it has seen, and the ear fears what it has heard. Halkano has seen and heard all this before. Right now, the whole scene appeared to him as if this was the first time that he had a realization.

***

Halkano dropped the charges against his mother. She left jail on the third day. The whole community, especially Halkano's supporters, were in total shock and still behaved as if they were in the mourning ceremony. They didn't talk about the campaign. There was nothing to talk about, and they knew he would not get any votes.

233

Votes or no votes, the people would never forget Halkano's name. How he would be judged by this community depended on several things, but no matter the outcome of this election, one thing was clear; Halkano's mind had changed for good, but for now, he would let the wound heal.

"I'll be back," he murmured. That night Halkano had a quiet dinner with his family. No one spoke at the table. It was the unspoken message that got through, and then Khadija broke the silence.

"Daddy, I'm okay now. Don't give up."

He looked at her innocent face wondering whether she meant winning the elections or fighting the girls' circumcision practice.

"No, sweetheart. I promise I won't." He paused for a moment. "You know what," he turned. "I'll fight this to the end. I don't care whether I will win this time or not, but I know one thing. For the next five years, I'll hunt down this barbaric habit and stop it." The silence continued.

The news of the outcome of the election reverberated in the distance. The radio announced it. People spread it by word of mouth. Some of Halkano's supporters thronged his home. They couldn't believe that he lost the election.

"As usual, the election was rigged, and they coerced the people to vote. I think we should not recognize the outcome. We have to fight it. They have used the same tactics and stuffed the ballot boxes, marked for Molu." Baraka lamented.

Halkano didn't reply. He had a lot of thinking to do and summed it with a traditional proverb. "Haadhaa yo dhugaan garaa guutatan." When one drinks bitter medicinal

mixture, one should fill the stomach. The proverb gave him
a consolation that he should fight for his convictions and
never give up.